William Alexander

St. Augustine's Holiday

And other Poems

William Alexander

St. Augustine's Holiday
And other Poems

ISBN/EAN: 9783744765374

Printed in Europe, USA, Canada, Australia, Japan

Cover: Foto ©Andreas Hilbeck / pixelio.de

More available books at **www.hansebooks.com**

ST. AUGUSTINE'S HOLIDAY

AND OTHER POEMS

BY

WILLIAM ALEXANDER, D.D., D.C.L.

BISHOP OF DERRY AND RAPHOE

LONDON

KEGAN PAUL, TRENCH & CO., 1, PATERNOSTER SQUARE

1886

[The two longest poems in this volume, and several other pieces, have not been printed before. For permission to publish the rest, my acknowledgments are due to the proprietors of *The Spectator*, *Good Words*, *The Contemporary Review*, *The National Review*, and *Macmillan's Magazine*.]

I very well know that he who would write anything in verse likely to live must surrender himself to verse passionately. and almost undividedly ; for poetry is as exacting as she is beautiful.   And indeed there was for myself a time, very long ago, when I was near believing that I had a call to consecrate myself to the sacred muse ; that I might possibly become one of the brethren who prophesy with harps, and are instructed in the songs of the Lord.   But a summons which I could not resist made me, to my surprise, a governor of the sanctuary and of the house of God.   Yet even now, late in my troubled day, I look back to my former purpose.   And here I gather together fragments mostly which (with three or four exceptions) I have had no sufficient time either to conceive deeply or to finish even after the measure of my own poor powers.   Some, I already know, care for the things such as they are, and think them not altogether worthy of death.   Perhaps God may enable me to say in the sweeter dialect dear to me long ago some things which I have failed to say in prose.   If so, I shall thank Him from my heart.   If not, the Church and the world will suffer no great wrong from me ; and, for myself, I do not much fear a whiff of sarcasm and the painless punish-ment of oblivion.

1.

TO ROBERT JOCELYN ALEXANDER.[*]

SUSPECTED all my life of poetry,
I come at last and make confession here.
Late, late, my son! in the autumn of my year.

ERRATA.

Page 17, line 4 from bottom, *for* "God's always is man's usual" *read* "God's usual is man's always."

,, 19, stanza 3, line 2, *for* "red-fruited" *read* "rich-fruited."

,, 46, line 3, *for* "has" *read* "hast."

,, 48, stanza 2, line 5, *for* "higher star" *read* "star higher."

,, 96, line 2 from bottom, *for* "life gives the life" *read* "Life gives the life."

,, 104, line 10, *for* "chance met" *read* "chance-met."

,, 133, lines 7 and 8 should form one line only.

,, 243, line 13, *for* "Dyonysus" *read* "Dionysus."

2.

Essayest thou, poet of a long-past morn,
A new forth-pouring of song's waves to try,
Song's wither'd blooms again on the fanes to tie?
Time was when from thy thought those waves seem'd
    borne

[*] See "Ishmael," by Robert Jocelyn Alexander, p. 219.
[†] Gen. xxxvii. 7.

I.

*TO ROBERT JOCELYN ALEXANDER.**

SUSPECTED all my life of poetry,
I come at last and make confession here.
Late, late, my son! in the autumn of my year,
I gather up my sheaves that scatter'd lie,—
Some faint far light of immortality
Falling upon my field, and the severe
Relentless winds whistling into mine ear—
"Gather thou up thy sheaves before thou die."
Sheaves! at that word I think of Israel's meadow
And valleys thick with corn.†   And on my lid
A proud tear trembles, as on his there did.
"These are my sheaves that rest, each on its shadow;
And all, along their little golden line,
Make their obeisance, O my son, to thine.

2.

Essayest thou, poet of a long-past morn,
A new forth-pouring of song's waves to try,
Song's wither'd blooms again on the fanes to tie?
Time was when from thy thought those waves seem'd
   borne

* See "Ishmael," by Robert Jocelyn Alexander, p. 219.
† Gen. xxxvii. 7.

Sunlit at once and strong, splendidly torn,
Their very fall a flash of victory.
Time was thy flowers were fresh as the morning sky,
To thee, perchance to others—now a scorn.
Two or three fibrous skeleton-leaves with story
Of some sweet summer day and things that died—
Two or three yellow foam-flakes for the glory,
Two or three bubbles for the big brimm'd tide.
—What if flowers breathe again before God's shrine,
Waves sound sonorous on a strand divine?

3.

I never yet heard music howe'er sweet,
Never saw flower or light, ocean or hill,
But a quick thought of something finer still
Touch'd me with sadness.　Never did I meet
Completest beauty but was incomplete,
Never view'd shapes half fair enough to fill
The royal galleries of my boundless will.
Never wrote I one line that I could greet
A twelvemonth after with a brow of fire.
Thus, then, with aim unreach'd, thought unexpress'd,
Unsatiated throbbings of desire,
I walk my way of life, and find no rest.
Thus beauty does not soothe me, and a cry
Of some deep want ends all my poesy.

4.

Lord! all my sins and negligences past,
Whereby, though fain, I am powerless to proclaim
Some great thing, worthy of Thy worthy Name,
Pardon.　And be Thy royal purple cast

O'er this vile vest ; and let the love thou hast
Flush this cold white to a red rose of shame.
And whilst Thou pardonest, Thou the very same,
My different sins, O pardon this the last —
This little song-shaft, full of motes that glance ;
This little gem, full of the flaw that pales ;
This little verse-book, full of verse that fails ;
This little music, full of dissonance ;
This little wild-rose, full of dust within ;
This little sin that is brimfull of sin.

CONTENTS.

I.

POEMS NARRATIVE, SACRED, AND REFLECTIVE.

II.

CHARACTERS, INSCRIPTIONS, Etc.

III.

WITHERED LAUREL LEAVES.

IV.

SONNETS.

V.

TRANSLATIONS.

* These translations from Victor Hugo were executed jointly by myself and my wife, Cecil Frances Alexander, chiefly in the year 1865.

I.

POEMS NARRATIVE, SACRED, AND REFLECTIVE.

ST. AUGUSTINE'S HOLIDAY.

(AUGUST TO DECEMBER, A.D. 386.)

SYNOPSIS.

St. Augustine retires to Cassiciacum to prepare for his baptism—His
company, especially his mother Monica, his natural son Adeodatus,
and the young poet Licentius—Augustine's Latin—Employment of
the party—Their studies and discussions—General condition of
Christian art and thought—Augustine's love of light; of the sea—
Speculations about disembodied spirits—Story of the Notary of
Uzala; of Gennadius—Comments upon the Psalter, especially the
Penitential Psalms; upon the Miracle of Cana—Licentius reads
Virgil aloud—His version of the tale of Dido—Speculations of the
young poet upon Virgil's condition in the world of spirits—Con-
clusion.

NOTE.—The books of St. Augustine which belong to this period are
these—"De Ordine," "De Vit. Beat.," "Contra Academ.," "De
Immort.," and the "Soliloquia." Augustine's own narrative has been
closely followed throughout this poem. The thoughts attributed to him
are generally to be found in his writings. Thus, his feeling for light is
beautifully marked in "Confess.," lib. x. 34. His appreciation of the
ocean will be doubted by no one who reads the following sentences.
"In cœli et terræ et maris multimodâ et variâ pulchritudine, in ipsius
quoque maris tam grandi spectaculo, cum sese diversis coloribus induit
velut vestibus, et aliquando viride atque hoc multis modis, aliquando pur-
pureum, aliquendo cœruleum est. Quàm porro delectabiliter spectatur

etiam quandocunque turbatur, et fit inde major suavitas." ("De Civ. Dei," xxii. 24). The stories of the Notary and of Gennadius are to be found in " Epp.," clviii. ix., so that the former at least is, literally speaking, an anachronism as it stands here. Licentius read Virgil to the party upon fine afternoons, substituting at times, apparently, poems of his own.

Now the sweet arrow of the Love divine
   Resistlessly had pierced Augustine's heart.
The flowers of speech he will no more entwine,
   Frequent no more the rhetorician's mart.
He gazes on the sun so long denied,
And the sun-gazer groweth sunny-eyed.

"His forehead, deep encrimson'd with the crown ;
   His lips, so full of grace, all deadly pale;
My Shepherd's wounded heart with woe cast down,
   My Shepherd's cheek cut with the cruel hail—
O'er what wild hills, in face of what a foam,
With what exultant arm He bore me home !

"Wholly for my poor love Himself He gave.
   A great gift for a miserable whole ;
An ocean for a little dying wave.
   And shall I offer him a divided soul,
Half of the mud that in the street doth lie,
If half the azure of the starlit sky ? "

Said Verecundus, " Thou art ill at ease.
   My farm lies north from here but a few leagues ;
Fair is its meadow-land, fair its chestnut trees.
   Go rest thee well from thy thoughts' long fatigues,
Thou and thy dearest." So Augustine went
On holiday to that green banishment—

For rest enfolded in that happy haunt,
    For time to meditate the Church's creed ;
For prayer, that when from the baptismal font
    He rises by regeneration freed,
The white life issuing thence his soul may win
To wear immaculate in a world of sin.

It was a little company of ten.
    Over them all was Monica gently set,
A flower of womanhood for those loving men.
    O winter flower, O faded violet,
By what rude fortune from thy garden toss'd,
Paled by what sun, discoloured by what frost?

With her a boy of fifteen summers came.
    Into the presence of the lad did pass
An influence from a climate as of flame ;
    And in those lustrous eyes of his there was
A tint of flowers and oceans far away
Amid the woods and waves of Africa.

Him evermore a shadow overhung,
    Not of the great Numidian forests born—
The prophecy of genius that dies young,
    The far cloud-film of a too radiant morn.
Ah ! they who early pass through one dark gate
Have looks like thine, thou young Adeodate !

Thou art of those who breathe with a strange smile
    The delicate words that only genius saith ;
Guests whom God spares us but a little while,
    For they are wanted in the land of death,
And leave but tracks of light that was not seen,
Hints of a golden land that might have been.

Hast thou no mother with a name to note?
   It is not written in the tenderest scroll
That love and recollection ever wrote,
   The perfected confession of a soul.
Into the dark she glides, a silent shame,
And a veil'd memory without a name.

And the world knoweth not what words she pray'd,
   With what long wail before the altar wept,
What tale she told, what penitence she made,
   What measure by her beating heart was kept,
Nor in what vale or mountain the earth lies
Upon the passionate Carthaginian's eyes.

Well that one penitent hath found such grace
   As to be silent in the silent years,
That no light hand hath lifted from her face
   The silver veil enwoven of her tears.
Well that one book at least, at least one sod,
Keeps close one tender secret of our God.

Well that the virgin saints of her may cry,
   " Our sister comes, mute after many tears—
Some anguish rounded by a victory
   Is hers, some calm after a storm of years.
O noble pity, that consoles her quite!
O large forgiveness, touching all to white !"

Next comes the laureate of the little throng,
   The young Licentius, whose deft art confers
Some grace upon the later Latin song—
   Waxwork, not marble, in hexameters—
Drawing in colours soft, but soon to cease,
A pastel for a proud old masterpiece.

But one moves aye among them as the chief—
  A thoughtful brow with saint engrav'd thereon.
And there was something of the Psalmist's grief,
  And of the inspiration of St. John,
And of the gravity that might beseem
The Plato of that little Academe.

Roman his speech, not as men talk'd at Rome.
  Here an apostle spake, and there a psalm,
And here philosophy had made its home.
  Passion and thought he pack'd in epigram,
Marring the stone of speech wherewith he wrought,
But perfecting the likeness of his thought.

O'er all he said there hung a subtle spell.
  For with him over sea a native art
He brought, an accent's glamour suiting well
  Magnificent barbarisms of the heart,
Learn'd by inhaling 'neath Numidian trees
Sunny solècisms of the provinces.

Four lakes, that made a fourfold heav'n below,
  Slept in that pleasant place, where Apennine
Grey-fissured meets the Alpine lines of snow ;
  Round it a symphony of light divine,
Red on the hill-side, gold along the plain,
The purpling cluster, and the yellowing grain.

One of those spots where busy hearts are still
  And world-worn natures quietly renew'd.
I see it now, hill rising over hill,
  The near ones crested with the olive wood,
And in the bluish distance, where morn breaks,
White behind all a line of snowy peaks.

Fair sped the days.   At noon, not overproud,
  They help'd the rustics with the vines or herd,
Which done, full oft the autumn-tide allow'd
  Sweet liberty for prayer or for the word,
Or for discourses grave, or readings made
From a page chequer'd by the chestnut shade.

Well for the men whose spirits try to scale
  The mountain peaks that overtop our lives.
There is a victory for them that fail,
  Defeat alone for him who never strives.
High themes wherewith to cope makes weak men strong:—
Well for the men who lived when thought was young.

Well for the men who lived in the long ago,
  They breath'd an ampler quietude than we ;
A few great books which they had time to know,
  Fresh as the untiring voices of the sea,
Made the old music that is ever new :—
Well for the men who lived when books were few.

Few books were with them ; but they were the best—
  The Epistles, Gospels, and prophetic scroll ;
The Psalter, too, wherein the ruggedest
  Of Latin takes to it a Hebrew soul,
And seems to yearn for music that may reach
The mysteries that lie beyond all speech.

Others, moreover, which no sage contemns,
  Nearest immortal mortals ever wrought,
Whose perfect words are the all-opulent gems
  That star the broad brows of the kings of thought,
Whose lines shall live as long as numbers flow—
Plato was there, Plotin, and Cicero.

They show in distance—chief the glorious Greek—
  The needle-point of truth enwrapt in mist,
Not the way leading to that difficult peak—
  Yet Plato preach'd magnificently Christ.
Yea, in each volume, and on every sod,
Whatever truth man troweth is of God.

Now, as I write, I seem to hear the kine,
  The rippling murmur of the little stream
That runs toward the bath through banks of vine,
  I see the moonlit hills rise like a dream—
The very leaf which autumn-tide brought low
In Lombardy a thousand years ago ;

And as it dropped insubstantive on the rill,
  And sinking help'd to break the brimming flow,
Set moving high discourse of fate and will,
  Proving that chance is God's incognito—
That chance, in Heaven's tongue order, interweaves
Vaster variety than waves and leaves.

And oft I meditate what round they made
  Of solemn usage and of stately form,
On what fair frame of visible things they stay'd ;
  What music fell in tears or rose in storm,
What soft imaginative rites they had,
With what investiture their faith they clad.

Not then the church rose visibly encrown'd.
  No mighty minster tower'd majestic yet.
No organ gave its plenitude of sound,
  And on the Alpine pinnacle was set
No carven King, whose crown is of the thorn,
No Calvary crimson in the southern morn.

No miracle of beauty and of woe
 Look'd from the wall, or for the rood was hewn,
No colour'd sunlight fell on the floor below.
 Under the silver of the Italian moon,
No visible throng of angels made their home
On the white wonder of the Gothic dome.

Yet, fed with inward beauty through the years,
 Much did the Church's mind anticipate
Of more majestic fanes, more tuneful tears,
 Simplicity more touching, nobler state.
—So the pale bud, where quietly it grows,
Dreams itself on superbly to the rose.

Questions by meditative wisdom ask'd
 Must wait for answer till the hour beseems;
Souls were as yet unborn severely task'd
 To give interpretation to such dreams;
Shapes by the master-hands as yet unfreed
Slept in the massive marble of the Creed.

The picture slept within the Gospel story;
 The music slept on psalms as on a sea;
In a dim dawn before its dawn of glory
 The poem slept, a thought that was to be.
The schoolmen's syllogisms, a countless train,
Were folded in that strong and subtle brain.

Christ said, "I need them." Out the colour sprang,
 The music wailed and triumph'd down the aisles,
With voices like the forest's poets sang,
 Invisible thoughts grew visible in smiles—
In smiles, and tears, and songs, and the exact
Majestic speech by centuries compact.

Sometimes at morning, or at eventide,
   Augustine look'd upon the lake and sky—
Not there the glory of light for which he sigh'd
   In all the autumn heaven of Italy.
" Poor shadows are ye—yea, but dimly bright
To me remembering that grander light.

  " Ah, light ! with its attendants all day long,
   Soothing and charming with a magic touch.
It passes not like every measured song,
   Its vast and variegated train is such,
Its omnipresent tide of silver flow,
The queen of all the colours of the bow.

  "O light ! which Isaac and which Jacob saw
   Falling upon the dim prophetic scroll,
When with closed eyes they taught the holiest law,
   The light that radiates from the luminous soul—
True light thou art of an unsetting sun,
And all who see thee and who love are one.

  " And they who turn away and this disdain
   Dwell in the flesh as in a shady place;
And yet of this whatever doth remain,
   Whate'er half-glooming glimmer touch their face,—
Yea, all that charms—is overflow divine,
And circumfulgence of that light of Thine.

  " Yet even here, upon this lawn of rest,
   I miss the splendour of my own far ocean,
The various robes which wondrously invest
   The evanescent moods of his emotion—
Green of a hundred shades and the fine fall
Of azure tint and pomp purpureal.

" Fair are these waters as these hills are fair,
   A fit enfolding for a rustic home ;
  But who their narrow beauty may compare
   With that majestic amplitude of foam ?
These azure reaches where the reeds scarce shake
The long calm silver of the Lombard lake,

" They cannot thunder with a voice like his,
   They cannot show the immeasurable line,
  They have no smoke of white foam o'er the abyss,
   No distances that infinitely shine,
No beat of a great heart, no pendulous swing,
No angry flap as of an eagle's wing.

" He has the magic swell, the tinkling fall,
   In drowsy days of truce, when skies are pure,
  Monotonous, incessant, musical ;
   And when his trumpets sound for war, the obscure
Æonian eloquence, the vast replies
Voluminous, the interminable sighs.

" The fierceness of him no man shall refrain—
   See him with all his water-floods astir,
  Like a great king, nigh dispossess'd of his reign,
   Staggering with fated hosts, a traveller
Against the wind upon his shoreward track,
His torn white hair tormentedly blown back.

" They have but one sweet look and steadfast tone ;
   Save when the tempest's battle may be set,
  The war of their white passion passes soon ;
   His the great epic, theirs the canzonet,
And the brief storm-bursts like an angry ode,
And the floods flashing like an episode."

Another while I seem'd to hear him speak :
   They had been calling back weird tales of ghosts,
Stories that grimly float in lands antique,
   Faint, fragmentary voices from grey coasts,
And the dim notices we sometimes have
From the far land that lies beyond the grave.

"Now, hear my stories. A few years ago
   Lived a boy-notary in Uzala town.
Letter'd full fair the sentences did flow
   From his quick pen. At first, youth's rosy crown
He wore with laughter ; then, the world abhorr'd,
Like Tertius ever writing in the Lord.

"He sicken'd in the feverish Autumn tide,
   And lay for sixteen days 'twixt death and life ;
But a few days before he gently died,
   And found his consolation after strife,
Faintly, half smiling, sang ere he went to rest,
'*Poculum tuum quám præclarum est.*'

"Then his own hand upon his forehead sign'd
   The holy cross, and on his lips did trace ;
And on the pillow where his head declined,
   Lay the sharp shadow of an old man's face—
So worn it was—but after a little while
Back came the boy-look and the innocent smile.

"Thereafter on the third day his friends came,
   To whom the tidings of his death was sent.
The priests he loved were gather'd to proclaim
   Redemption's sweet and awful sacrament.
Now two days later was a vision seen.
There rose a palace from a meadow green ;

"From it funereal music sounded slow,
　　A faint sweet scent went out upon the air ;
　The great gates open'd noiselessly ; and lo !
　　Its halls and floors were golden everywhere,
And passing stately out with sound of chants
An old man stood with two white pursuivants.

"And, 'Lift me the boy's body for awhile
　　Heavenward,'he said, 'for heavenward was his walk.'
　Which done, for peradventure half a mile,
　　Rose-trees appear'd, a bud on every stalk.
Buds of the roses red and white were they—
Such buds are virgins call'd in Africa.

"And when the priest, his father, came that night,
　　And threw himself in prayer on the boy's grave,
　Lo ! in the glory of a silver light
　　A thousand rosebuds lay on it, and gave
Such attestation as mute things may give
To those whose lives unstain'd by passion live.

"Of roses, my Licentius ! singing next,
　　With Horace sing not, myrtled at his wine ;
　Be not thy verse with paynimry perplex'd,
　　But raise thy poesy to strains divine,
And tell how fitly angel hands let fall
Such virgin gifts for spirits virginal.

"Now for a graver tale.　In youth I knew
　　Gennadius, a physician.　Over sea
　He came to Africa, and not a few
　　Brought with him of the youth of Italy ;
Preferring for his science and his home
The marble streets of Carthage to his Rome.

" From groping in the mechanism of our frame
   There was a faltering in the good man's faith ;
Not once or twice to him the question came,
   Whether for man a life were after death,
Haunting him as he thought of heart and brain,
And track'd the dim tremendous path of pain.

" Yet still he pray'd, ' O life of every life,
   O truth believed in first, then understood,
Give me the prize that is not won by strife ;
   Give me faith's sweet translucent certitude.'
Then a voice came to him o'er sleep's soft sea,
Saying, ' Arise, Gennadius, follow me.'

" Him following, to a certain place he fared,
   Where on the right there rose a dulcet strain
Beyond all sweetness he had ever heard ;
   And as he listen'd to that soft refrain,
' This,' said the spirit who him had in trust,
' This is the music of the perfect just.'

" So he awoke, and cried, ' A dream at best.'
   But the next night the very same young man
Came, saying, ' Gennadius, thou rememberest—
   Answer, and I will help thee as I can—
The things thine eyes and ears did lately take ;
Saw'st thou and heard'st in vision, or awake ?

" ' Can thy cold skill or cunning scalpel find
   A way to that impenetrable lair,
The life intense of the impalpable mind ?
   Or canst thou tell thy purblind scholars where
The ear that hears the swell as of the sea,
The wondrous eyes wherewith thou seest me ?

" 'So when thy body lieth in its bed,
    Be it the ocean wave, or burial sod,
When thou art of the sleepers men call dead,
    That in thee which is deathless may see God.
There may be gloom or gleam for the soul's eyes
In doleful dells, or bowers of Paradise.' "

Often he took the Psalter in his hand,
    And turn'd to pages blister'd long with tears,
The balm of broken hearts in every land,
    The consolation of a thousand years ;
And nobly bold told penitents their bliss,
In gentle images perchance like this—

"Look when thou walkest by the winter strand,
    Hath it befallen thee, that through the grey
Of the sea mist, into thy very hand,
    Floated a snow-white bird through the salt spray,
Fair, but deep wounded, bubbling from its beak
A thin red foam, with faint infantine shriek ?

" Which noting, to thyself thou mad'st a dirge—
    ' There is no healing in this hand of mine ;
Here must thou die, by the unpitying surge ;
    Not in the long blue distances divine,
Not in thy little happiness upborne
On seas refulgent with the rosy morn.'

" Such, and so sorely wounded, floating in,
    Are penitents beside the sea of time :
Such, and so deep, the crimson stain of sin,
    The scar we bear in this ungentle clime.
But lo ! a healing Hand our wound above,
Strong as eternity, and soft as love.

"And a sweet voice that unto us hath lent
　A new beginning and a nobler flight.
So to poor hearts He gives incontinent
　A larger liberty of golden light ;
Makes more than expiation for our fault,
And arches over us His bluest vault,

"Saying, ' I charge thee, O my wounded bird,
　Soar nearer to the heaven where'er thou art ;
Let all the breezes by thy plumes be stirr'd ;
　I heal thee through and through, O bleeding heart !
I ask thy song, and give thee voice to sing ;
I bid thee soar, and give thee strength of wing.

" ' What I command I give my mourners still,
　Give the delight that doth the victory gain ;
Give first, and then command them as I will,
　Sweet penitence taking pleasure in its pain.
I bid thee set those psalms of sorrow seven
To the allegro of the airs of Heaven.' "

And yet another time methought one read
　The gentle miracle of the Marriage Feast.
"Ours be the sweetness of the wine," he said,
　"The bridal benediction of our Priest ;
And in the silence of our hearts be heard
The voiceless words of Him who is the Word.

" Each vineyard is a purple curtain screen,
　Whereon God's colours we may ever trace ;
God's always is man's usual, and is seen
　Paled by too constant light to common place ;
And scarcely do our drowsy hearts revere
The miracle of vintage every year.

C

"God is not bound by laws Himself has made ;
　　Water is not less wonderful than wine ;
　　God's living finger weaves a pattern'd braid,
　　　Yet in full liberty of love divine,
And still free notes of a new music dwell
In Heaven's sweet novelty of miracle.

"Lo ! the world's gifts are goodliest at first—
　　The rapturous enjoyment, the rich sense,
　　The revelling draught—thereafter the fierce thirst,
　　　The dark'ning sky, the passionate impotence.
But Thou hast kept Thy light for our eclipse—
Kept Thy good wine for pale and dying lips."

And once, when near its end their idlesse drew,
　　It chanced the afternoon was mild and fine.
　　The Master cried, "What ho ! the sky is blue.
　　　Come, poet, read the verse thou call'st divine.
Nay, and I will not blame thee overmuch
If thou mix with it thine own gentle touch.

"Thy Virgil bring.　With him thou shalt bring flowers,
　　Odours emparadised in some fadeless phrase.
　　Thou shalt set bees a-humming in the bowers,
　　　And make us weep for old immortal days ;
And, pagan though he be, yet shall we bless
God's gift in him of exquisite tenderness.

"Fling, then, o'er us the great magician's spell,
　　Read with meet cadence while the eve is clear
　　Tell o'er again what our hearts know so well.
　　　The moonlit sea shall quiver as we hear—
In one six-beated line a tale be stored,
A garden gather'd in one perfect word."

To whom Licentius.   " Lately I was thinking
    Of the delicious love-tale Virgil wrought—
Out of his cup my spirit had been drinking ;
    Rather, I sank into his ocean thought.
And with the tide I swam that summer sea,
And all its waves grew buoyant under me.

" There was a murmur in my ears and heart,
    Whereof the larger music came from him ;
But of mine own there was a little part,
    Little indeed to his, and harsh and dim.
Of Homer's mighty song and high intent
Sonorous echo, theft magnificent

" He made ; but ah ! I marr'd whate'er I stole—
    He the red-fruited scion, the stem I
Of the poor pomegranate, lending to the whole
    Only the red tint of my poverty—
He like the bird's white wing above the river,
I the white shadow that can reach it never.

" Listen ! I breath'd our soft Numidian air ;
    I saw Elissa to the hunting go ;
The golden-netted sunshine of her hair
    Flicker'd in sunshine as it fell below.
The golden baldrick flung she round her breast,
The golden fibula clasp'd her purple vest.

" With yellow jasper stone his sword hilt starr'd,
    He how majestic, like a prince indeed,
How stately she, how regal of regard !
    A huntress on her white Massylian steed.
And, though the jocund morning waxes late,
Herself impatient makes her lover wait,—

"Who looks like Phœbus, when he Cynthus treads,
   After the Lycian snows and streams ice-mute,
Walking with murmurous rush of river-beds;
   While heav'n is silver o'er him, and underfoot
Anemones spring, and daffodils are born
For golden tassels to his bugle horn.

"Ah me! how beautiful to her he seem'd,
   To whom such fascination there was given.
The mountain-tops whereon his boyhood dream'd,
   Had forests haunted by the hosts of Heaven.
Out of the sunset sky ablaze with flame,
Out of the silver silences he came;

"Came with the music of the Idalian pines
   Round him, with whisper'd message from the star,
His mother's herald o'er the mountain lines,
   Until dawn steeps her pure pale primrose bar
In rosiest colour'd radiance ever born
Out of the ivory palaces of morn;—

"Came with such touch of moonlight on his sail,
   From such resplendent distances of foam,
With all the loveliness of such a tale,
   The spell of such a visionary home;
And finely floated round that princely form
A mystery of the battle and the storm.

"Full soon she sobs, 'Stay if my prayer avails;
   Train me to bear the last long parting thus;
Stay till our Afric wild-flow'rs fill the dales,
   Till yon waves look less strange and dangerous,
Till I shall discipline this poor heart so
That with the swallows I may let thee go.

"'Ah ! an thou fleest, then my wraith be found
　　Where'er thy fateful footsteps yet shall stand—
My very shadow shall be gold-encrown'd,
　　My very shadow shall be sad and grand ;
My shadow haunt thee on each sea and lawn,
Mute in the moonlight, dying in the dawn.'

" Perchance he would have stay'd, but not in vain
　　The calling to our purpose on us lies.
Our lives are links in a remorseless chain.
　　Of what avail to her that his heart sighs
' Elissa, and a Carthaginian home,'
When Heaven and all its influence will have Rome ?

" Soon this hath passed.　The parting all is o'er,
　　And all her passionate reproach of him,
And all the watching from the salt seashore
　　Of the sail fading o'er the ocean rim—
Of the sail fading on the cruel sea,
On the false wave not half so false as he.

" Night, gentle night, rush'd from the Afric sky.
　　Head under wing the birds of wave and air
Slept, hushing all their sweet small poesy.
　　If we have our forgetfulness of care,
So have those little hearts in bower and brake,
And the still dreamland of the starlit lake.

" But she her fiery bed premeditates,
　　And '·Let him see the smoke, a far off breath,'
She wails ; ' a blur on Summer's lustrous gates,
　　And bear with him the omen of my death—
Ah no ! my poor heart be, till it wax dim,
A taper on a shrine, and burn for him.

"'And if so be that Herè in her ruth
  Send Iris with the hopes and hues of heav'n
To hang above my death, I pray in sooth
  That half the sweetness may to him be given,
And half my rainbow melt away in rose
And violet on the ocean where he goes.'

"This passed away—and then meseem'd to tread
  The underworld in visionary sleep.
Æneas-like I visited the dead.
  Behold! a spirit pass'd, who seem'd to weep
Not hopelessly. 'Young Poet!' did he say,
Men call'd me Maro while I saw the day.

"'Each of us poets hath his proper gift;
  Not all the gift to use the gift aright.
Red cups of battle or of wine they lift
  Wildly, and stain what should be lily white.
Each bloom has thus its cankerworm within,
Each splendid line is thus a splendid sin.

"'And others sang high strains with mean intent
  Or for the tyrant of their little time,
Or gave to hatred what for love was meant;
  Less than immortal made immortal rhyme,
So that the satire with the years has grown
A fossil scorpion with a sting of stone.

"'The Latin tongue was lent me at my will.
  Lo! the flowers fade upon the summer leas
The storm of battle passes, and is still;
  But sorrow is a deeper thing than these—
Sorrow for human things lasts through the years
I was the first that chose the gift of tears.

" ' I used it as an instrument to express
  Beyond all battle camps, and courts of kings,
The majesty of human tenderness,
  Sweet ruth for the vicissitudes of things—
The subtle pathos, the magnetic touch,
The broken voice that tells the heart so much.

" ' Once the dim prophecies floating round the earth
  I gather'd—thornless roses, stormless seas,
Meadows in blossom for a better birth,
  Mother and child, *nova progenies*—
All this I twined for all the race of man
In higher strains than aught Sicilian.

" ' And is it nothing that I taught all this,
  That through the world's confusion sweetly smiled
Before me the conception of our bliss,
  The happiest Mother, the divinest Child,
That scarcely once or twice did touch impure
Fall on my virginal emportraiture?'

" Then with low voice he ask'd, ' And is there hope?
  Or must I wander always—lost, lost, lost?'
Out like a rose the dawn began to ope,
  This side and that the clouds were crimson cross'd,
And manifold voices round us seem'd to say,
' Yea, there is hope, but it is far away.'

" Ah! not so far—for low and winning sweet,
  ' *Venite, invenietis,*' some one said ;
Like breath of balm upon the heart it beat.
  Light ran along the region of the dead.
The echoes multiplied from east to west,
' *Venite ad me omnes—suave est.*' "

Licentius ceased.   To Elissa's tale at even
  A hundred times within the twenty years
Augustine's tender heart had duly given
  The tributary offering of his tears.
Yet,—while the boy's big drops of ruth he chid,
The salt dew trembled on the Master's lid.

And Monica thought how first she read the tale
  In her Numidian home at eventide,
Thought of Æneas with each sunlit sail,
  Thought of Elissa with each wave that died.
The saint perhaps condemned it, but alas !
The woman sigh'd, and said how sweet it was.

As to the boy's deep ruth and tender prayer
  For Virgil, be there silence grave and wise.
The mother of the Master was aware
  How the first woodland walk through which we rise
To the precipitous mountain peak of truth
Is love—the sunlit heresy of youth.

The holiday is o'er—the rest is done.
  Cassiciácum lies in sunny mist ;
They turn toward it, praying every one,
  " To Verecundus do thou give, O Christ !
For that sweet rest beneath the happy skies
The fadeless greenery of Thy Paradise."

Never was yet to-day whose incompleteness
  Fail'd not in somewhat of the bliss it brought,
Till it inherited the dim faint sweetness,
  The immaculate azure of the sky of thought ;
Till we baptized the dead hours far away
By the ethereal name of yesterday.

So " My one holiday," oft the old man cried ;
　" When shall the Bishop's holiday come again ? "
When the fierce Huns are on the mountain-side,
　And he lies sick to death in August ; when
The cactus flowers of Hippo 'neath the blue
Are steep'd with crimson blood-drops through and through ;

When through the date groves in the scarce-lit dales
　Over the Seybous and his dreaming calms,
The importunate sweetness of the nightingales
　Comes to the old man falling asleep with psalms ;
And, a thin thread of scarlet, morning breaks
Silently on the Atlantéan peaks.

AN OLD VOLUME OF SERMONS.

SYNOPSIS.

Study of the Song of Songs—Two schools of interpretation—The first
represented by M. Renan's " Le Cantique "—The vaudeville theory
—The second represented by St. Bernard's LXXXVI. Sermons
upon Canticles—The influence of the book upon the saint's life—
His early days—His mother Aleth—His renunciation of the world
and of the worldly side of the Church—He brings with him his whole
family, including his father, Sir Tescelin, and his sister, Humbeline
—Clairvaux—Spiritual power of St. Bernard's teaching—Visit of
St. Malachy, Archbishop of Armagh, to Clairvaux—His death there
—Death of his brother Girard—Incapacity of nature to console—
St. Bernard's sermon on Cant. i. 5—The Pope visits Clairvaux—
Simplicity of his reception—Sermon on Cant. ii. 16—Conclusion
—Cant. v. 2, 5—Summary of the spiritual interpretation. ,

NOTE.—In the composition of this poem, I have constantly availed
myself of the interesting and accurate notices (*Note sur Fontaine-les-
Dijon, patrie de St. Bernard*, par l'Abbé Chenevet) and other local
papers in the fourth volume of Migne's edition of St. Bernard's works,
pp. 1621–1661.

The death of St. Malachy at Clairvaux took place in 1148. St.
Bernard has written the archbishop's life, which is here closely followed. The visit of Pope Innocent to Clairvaux was many years earlier,
in 1131. Ernald's account has been carefully used. " A pauperibus
Christi, non purpurâ et bysso ornatis, nec cum deauratis Evangeliis

occurrentibus, sed pannosis agminibus scopulosam bajulantibus crucem, non tumultuantium classicorum tonitruo, non clamosâ jubilatione, sed suppressâ modulatione affectuosissime susceptus est. Flebant episcopi, fleba tipse summus Pontifex; omnes mirabantur congregationis illius gravitatem. Nihil in ecclesiâ illâ videbat Romanus quod cuperet. Nihil in oratorio nisi nudos viderunt parietes. Solennitas non cibis, sed virtutibus agebatur. Panis ibi autopyrus pro simila, pro careno sapa, pro rhombis olera, pro quibuslibet deliciis legumina ponebantur. Si forte piscis inventus est, domino Papæ appositus est, et aspectu, non usu, in commune profecit" (St. Bernard, "Vita," lib. ii., Auctore Ernaldo., ap. opp. S. Bernard, iv. 272). Passages from the Sermons on the Canticles are freely transferred to the poem. Mr. Frederic Harrison's beautiful and appreciative article on St. Bernard did not reach me until my verses were almost finished. Of such a writer one can but say, "Cum talis sis, utinam noster esoes."

I READ the " Song of Songs "—I thought it pure,
　　The very flame of the full love of God;
And over it there hung the clear obscure
　　Of Syrian night, and scents were blown abroad
Whose very names breathe on us mystic breath—
Myrrh, and the violet-striped habatseleth.

　　Strange words of beauty hung upon mine ear—
　　Semada, that is scent and flower in one
Of the young vine-blooms in the prime of the year;
　　Senir, Amana, Carmel, Lebanon,
Eloquent of rivers and of mountain trees,
Dim in the Oriental distances.

　　And purple paradise of pomegranate flowers,
　　Kopher, kinnamon, balsam, wealth of nard,
And things that thickets fill in summer hours,
　　Blue as a sky white-clouded, golden-starr'd,
Whereby we may surmise not far from thence
Mountains of myrrh and hills of frankincense.

I read the Hebrew late into the night;
 At last the lilies faded, and the copse
Had no more fragrance, and I lost delight,
 As when in some sweet tongue a poem stops,
Half understood—yet being once begun,
Our hearts are strangely poorer when 'tis done.

Two volumes lay before me. One a tome
 Which heretofore for years had stood between
Tender Augustine, terrible Hierome;
 And the last Father's name was duly seen
In faded letters betwixt leather thongs—
"Saint Bernard's Sermons on the Song of Songs."

The other, fresh from Paris, "Le Cantique,"
 Look'd a thin volume of a new romance.
Yet did I pray, "O Spirit whom I seek,
 Teach me by which of these two lights of France,
The unbegun Beginning I may reach,
Thy sweetest novelty in oldest speech."

So the two books I read; the first whereof,
 A drama of earth's flame this song did deem—
Five acts with epilogue, tale of true love,
 Shepherd and vine-dresser—such shiyr shyriym
Idyllic as Theocritus might trill—
Say rather, a soft Hebrew vaudeville.

Solomon sweeps by with threescore mighty men,—
 Poor dove, all fluttering in the falcon's beak,
So foully carried from her quiet glen !
 He flashes on with her so sweetly weak,
Elderly, evil-eyed, and evil-soul'd,
Scented and cruel in a cloud of gold.*

* Cant. iii. 6-11. M. Renan, "Étude sur le Cantique," pp. 30,
31, 190, 191.

To the accursèd palace they have come.
  Dresses like rainbows float through the Harem.
To the faint plash of fountains never dumb
  Are sung wild songs of earth's unholiest flame.
The large-eyed odalisks are lolling there;
The tambour taps, and bounds the bayadère.

  Ah! as in dreams her shepherd singing stands:
  " Arise, my love, my fair one, come away;
The winter has pass'd over into lands
  Whose heritage is rain, whose heavens are grey.
Flow'rs for my flow'r, the turtle's voice is heard—
It is the green time for the singing bird.

  " The exhalation of the vine-bloom flows
  On the rich air.   Why is my white dove mute
In the cleft of the rock?   Behold, the fig-tree throws
  Her aromatic heart into her fruit.
Save for me only spring is everywhere.
O let me hear thee from thy mountain stair."

  Which hearing, in her heart she hums her lilt,
  Learnt long ago of some dark vine-dresser.
Sing it, O maiden, whensoe'er thou wilt.
  The vine-leaf shadow o'er thee is astir—
" Let not the little foxes from thee 'scape,
Spoiling our vines that have the tender grape."

  And so, O peasant girl, be won for wife.
  No young Theresa of the Hebrews thou;
Yet an illusion traverses thy life
  Which gives ideal light to thy dark brow,
Which makes home beautiful, and proudly sings
Songs of defiant purity to kings.

And if no ecstasy lights up thy face,
   No flame of seraphim consumes thy heart;
If thou hast natural truth, not heavenly grace;
   At least, O sunburnt Shulamite! thou art
A tender witness to a purer lot
In the base centuries when love was not.

I smiled a moment.   Then a discontent
   Filled me with grief and spiritual shame.
"Where then?" I cried, "is the old ravishment,
   The ointment pour'd forth of the Holiest Name?
This song was once as fair for souls to mark
As the sod fresh cut to the prison'd lark—

" A daisied sod whereon the bird in rapture
   Quivers, remembering a little while
The large inheritance before his capture,
   When from some azure and unmeasured mile
He rain'd down music, where the shadows pass
From the white cloud-sails o'er the glittering grass."

And a voice said, "Take thou the other book;
   Therewith the life of the great Abbot scan.
Behold its peace and purity, and look!
   He guides the restless intellect of man—
All streams that from all monasteries part,
And the king's council, and the woman's heart.

" He cleaves through heresy with one bright word,
   Weak with the weakest, stronger than the strong,
   Holds love a sharper weapon than the sword,
   Helpeth all them to right who suffer wrong;
And as he walks the world, in street or dell,
The dry earth blossoms into miracle."

I read the double columns thro' and thro',
   Till the Saint's eyes look'd at me from the line.
Methought the heav'n above the book was blue,
   And love's green land before me lay divine ;
And, " Hearken to him," said a voice to me,
Cor meum vulnerasti is the key,

   " Whereto the riddle is no riddle more.
     The Bride and Spouse he ever doth rehearse,
One epithalamium sings he o'er and o'er—
     Christ and the Church ; and for the measured verse
Forbidden true Cistercians, as he knows,
Takes a saint's vengeance in impassion'd prose."

   " What time the world in winter morn is white,
     The prints upon the snow are for thine eye
A record of the chronicles of night—
     Such snow be this sweet song, a mystery
On whose white surface thou may'st see the faint
And heavenward traces of a pilgrim saint."

   " Draw me," One saith.   " We will run after Thee."
     The Boy's eyes open'd on a golden land—
Forest and chase, river and lilied lea,
     And steeds to rein, and vassals to command,
And the light rippled in the summer air
In softer gold on Bernard's chestnut hair.

   Full shy he was, and grave and sweet of speech,
     Of skill in riding and running at the ring,
And ever ready to give right to each ;
     Which seeing, his father smiled upon the thing,
And said to Aleth, with a proud bright glance,
" What if our boy be Burgundy's first lance ?

" What if he wed a maid of high estate ?
　　With her a castle by broad acres girt.
He that will greatly rise must wisely wait ;
　　So I will mail him in his battle-shirt,
And send him to the wars, that he may be
All that beseems a knight of his degree."

But Lady Aleth, faintly smiling, said,
　　" Ah, this boy Bernard is of other stamp.
But yesterday he sigh'd, ' I will not wed.
　　Mother, I hate the revel and the camp,
The drops of blood upon our castle walks,
And the fierce beauty of my father's hawks.

" ' I will no poesy of earthly loves,
　　I put from me all Ovid's magic spell ;
Two voices hold me only--one the dove's,
　　The Spouse's one, in God's sweet canticle ;
And my heart hears one singing every day,
" Arise, my love, my fair one, come away." ' "

" What must be, must," replied Sir Tescelin.
　　" Squires carry knights' spurs germinant at their heel ;
Young priest becomes young prelate without sin ;
　　If Bishop Bernard at the altar kneel,
Were he less saint, an if his saintship gain
A glorious abbacy, a broad domain ? "

But " Nay," quoth she, " nor may this come to pass.
　　Now, I will tell thee what is in his heart
In his own words, yesterday after Mass :
　　' Mother, a voice is calling me apart ;
All the day long it sayeth within me,
" Draw me, O Lord ; we will run after Thee."

"'Sometimes meseems the trump of Judgment sounds;
    Sometimes God pierceth me, and sometimes wins,
With great attraction of the five sweet Wounds,
    With fierce light flashing on my little sins.
That which I yearn for is not court nor strife,
But the beginning of a saintly life—

"'The lore that scarcely may be learn'd aright
    From any parchment on a dusty shelf,
The stern self-discipline of God's true knight,
    Who bravely wars the warfare against self,
Bow'd in a penitence at the bleeding Feet,
Whereof the very bitterness is sweet.

"'Sinful with all the sinful I would go
    To the one heart human, and yet divine;
Nor lavish all my love on aught below,
    Nor bow too deeply at another shrine,
As if in all heav'n's host there were for such
A truer pity or a tenderer touch.

"'Nothing from self, all from His perfect Name—
    To say the good thing in me is mine own,
That were as if the chamber wall should claim
    The golden sunbeam shimmering on the stone;
That were to drain the ocean with thy lips,
Or turn back Jordan with thy finger-tips.

"'Perchance our Church has too much of the earth;
    Our abbots, peradventure, are too rich;
We ask too often—"What is the see worth?"
    Forget the fane to overgild the niche.
Give me no jewell'd mitre, no red garb,
No bowing vassals, and no milk-white barb.

" ' Nay, over-gaudy grown with time that grows,
　　Religion robes herself in rainbow dyes.
　Ah, sighs and tears ! the sighs she doth enclose
　　In bubbles, and the tears she petrifies ;
And pomp enwrappeth in a golden pall
The rich rigidity of ritual.

" ' First, let the soul be beautiful within ;
　　Then the soul's beauty duly shall create
　Form, colour, harmony, to awe and win—
　　Outward from inward as inseparate
As music from the river when it flows,
Shadow from light, or fragrance from the rose.

" ' My portion be the austere and lowly fane,
　　The quiet heart that praises ere it sings,
　The genuine tears that fall like timely rain,
　　The happy liberty from outward things,
The wing that winnoweth the ample air,
The heaven's gate touch'd by the soft hand of prayer.

" ' The sunshine-veinèd vintage stored for years,
　　Quaff'd with quaint laughter in the refectóry,
　Of this I will have none—but tender tears,
　　The lore of saints, the spiritual glory,
The brotherhood, the cross whereof one saith,
No ill thing glides where'er it shadoweth.

" ' I saw a great Cistercian abbey rise,
　　And out of heaven there fell a voice divine—
　" Enter in, son of Aleth ! on this wise,
　　Reformer of the Order, all is thine.
Rise, come away ; " whereon I did rejoice
In the irresistible music of that voice.

" ' " But first," I pleaded, " Lord, thou know'st I have
    Six brothers and a sister, in all seven.
Lover of souls, O infinite to save,
    Give me all these for company in heaven.
Draw them in also ;" and then bolder grown—
"I would be saved, O Lord, but not alone."

" ' And then I saw sculptured above the gate
    " *The vale of Wormwood is a vale of Light ;* "
And outside there was wailing, war, and hate,
    And a voice of agony out in the black night ;
But in I drew the six from that wild teen,
And last of all my fair-hair'd Humbeline.

" ' Then, thee, my mother, too, I drew thee in—
    Not fair as thou art now, but cold and pale.
O gentlest heart that ever conquer'd sin !
    O Christ's sweet Shulamite in the nun's white veil !
And on thy lips I laid the Host that hour,
And rain'd down tears on thee, my winter flower !

" ' And last of all my father.   I could hear
    What were the things that to himself he said :
" Will he not leave me for another year ?
    Can he not wait till the old man is dead ?
I would much rather die in my old room
Than in a cloister of Cistercian gloom.

" ' " I would much rather rest with my rough race,
    Close to the altar, in the church I built ;
I would the villagers should see my face
    And Aleth's marble under a canopy gilt,
Whispering—*This was a joyous knight and just,*
They say he is a thousand years in dust.

" ' " A thousand years he wears his shirt of mail,
    And his good hound is couchant at his feet ;
If that tough cheek of his be deathly pale,
    'Tis but the stone that makes such paleness meet,
And in his calm eye come what tide soe'er
Is sure regard of everlasting prayer.

    " ' " Yet is it certain what monks say—that souls
    Are lost in circles of light as in a flood,
That the saints worship day and night in stoles,
    Posed without end in marble attitude,
Or like the angels on a vestment shown
Stitch'd in a sapphire prayer before the throne?

    " ' " All the night long Sir Tescelin looks to the east,
    And the sweet lady by him never stirs.
But when the thin moon wanes down to her least,
    And dawn plays faint about his marble spurs,
Doth he not sometimes seem to waken?   Hist!
Doth the white falcon flutter on his fist?

    " ' " All the night long he prays, I have no doubt,
    When o'er the October moon the big clouds whirl,
And ever and anon she cometh out
    With fleece of rainbow and of mother o' pearl—
Her flying touch some minutes' space being still
White on the broken waters by the mill.

    " ' " But is not yon stiff hound about to yawn ?
    The lady to hear mass as is her wont?
Are not the rustics going to the lawn
    To see the gallants gathering for the hunt?
Ah ! this is idle talk, for well know I
Such things are not in that eternity.

" ' " But what and if my appointed time draws near,
   And I and all I have is doom'd to death ;
And what and if for all that I hold dear,
   The grace of the fashion of it vanisheth ;
And if this poor old heart at last must go
Like a tree broken by its weight of snow—

" ' " May I not die upon my Aleth's bed,
   With shadows of the long familiar trees
Making their chequer-work upon my head,
   Amid the humming of my yellow bees,
Where to the sun my peacocks spread their stains
Upon my castle terrace of Fontaines ? "

" ' Nay, for all that, dear father, at the fold
   Thou knockest.   Thy son openeth, and from heaven
A voice falls musical for thee : " Behold
   Thou and thy children whom the Lord has given.
Listen to Bernard's voice, and enter in,
Sweet Lady Aleth, stout Sir Tescelin ! " ' "

The Abbey stands in Clairvaux.   Bernard speaks
   From the stone pulpit by the brethren hewn,
Of the " Name," or " Lilies," or " Till morning breaks,"
   Making discourse till late in the afternoon ;
Pathos and majesty in his speech were blent,
Sweetness magnetic and magnificent.

" Whence skillest thou ? " his brother Girard said,
   " To trace these love-links ever feast and fast ?
Thou hast not much perused the deathless dead ;
   Yet shall these words of thine for ever last,
Little in space, but sparks of living flame,
Little indeed, but roses all the same.

" And happy we, to whom in thee are given
   Such sweets both new and old, such lily flowers,
Such precious antepast of feasts of heaven.
   High joy for us of these monastic bowers,
To gather on this green Burgundian sod
Thy pale gold honey, O thou bee of God."

"I know not brother," and the Abbot smiled ;
   "Yet thou rememberest the forest well.
A few years since the snow was on it piled. ·
   Thou knowest how often ere the vesper bell,
My meditation was prolonged—and ye
Said it was sweet—perchance in flattery.

" Nathless the young narcissus snow-drops came
   With spring (our rustics call them ' angels' tears ') ;
A hundred greens were out, no two the same ;
   The happy promise given by young years
For ever, and for evermore belied,
Lit the young leaves, and smiled some hours, and died.

"So came the spring to Burgundy.   Then spoke
   A voice from out the depths where earth's life stirs.
The ' Song of Songs ' reads well under the oak—
   A soft interpretation sigh the firs ;
And God's good Spirit taught me what to teach
Through the uncountable whispers of the beech.

" From the anemones pass'd to me my thought,
   Through the woods trembling in their thin white robe.
A subtler music came to me unsought
   Upon the washing of the murmurous Aube ;
And the long sunset rays on the great boles
Wrote me the comment of the holy souls.*

* " Nullos se magistros habuisse nisi quercus et fagos joco illo
gratioso inter amicos dicere solet."   (S. Bernard, Vita, opp. iv. 240.)

" For were the Canticle a passion strain,
　　And if it spake of aught beneath the sky,
　Then from its images thy heart could gain
　　A love-snatch only, or a botany ;
Whereas, he finds in it who truly tries,
Strength from the strong, and wisdom from the wise.

" Here is the ocean of the love divine
　　For the whole Church.　What smaller than a sea
　Can hold a sea ? and yet thy heart and mine
　　Reflection of it hath for thee and me,
As one clear bubble sphereth for the eye
The azure amplitude of wave and sky.

" And this love-strain is never over-told.
　　When God Himself is our musician, say,
　Wilt thou correct Him to a strain less bold,
　　And teach the mighty Master how to play ?
Two, two alone can hear these tender things—
The soul that listens, and the soul that sings."

Late, late, in the October afternoon,
　　The monks sat listening spell-bound in the choir ;
　The voice went ringing on, a lovely tune,
　　A touch of pathos, or a shaft of fire.
The sunset flared blood-red, the wild marsh hen
Shriek'd through the long reed lances of the fen.

Within was spring.　Voice to low breezes set
　　Through the greenwood, over the mountain's brink—
　Voice of Christ's dove, His undefilèd—yet,
　　Not so much sweet itself of song, I think,
As the soft sign whereby we understand
That all things sweet are gathering in the land.

" O that some saint might come to us, and teach
　　From his rich certainty our poor *perhaps !*
Yea, by his death preach what I cannot preach—
　　How earth's hopes scare at last, as when there taps
Some broken branch of bloom through storm and rain,
Like death's white finger on the window-pane."

Scarce was the sermon done, the blessing o'er,
　　A train of horsemen halted at the gate.
" My Lord the Abbot," said the janitor,
　　" One like an angel comes to us full late,
Primate of a green island o'er the sea ;
His name, too, is an angel's—Malachy."

Four or five days flow'd on in fair discourse ;
　　Gracious his speech and stately his regard.
Oft would he warn them with prophetic force
　　That he was come to them to meet the Lord.
He rode to Clairvaux in October mist,
The Feast-day of St. Luke the Evangelist.

Something of fever flush'd his pallid cheek ;
　　To Bernard mournfully a little while
Out of his spirit's trouble did he speak
　　Of certain tribesmen in his restless isle.
" Patience," he cried, " that tree of hidden root,
And bitter rind, that hath so sweet a fruit,

" Be the good guerdon of the bishop's heart,
　　The turbulent sheep who shepherds in that land.
Full often must he bear, with breaking heart,
　　The long ingratitude, the plot well plann'd,
The deep suspicion hid with laughing eye,
The poison'd dagger sheath'd with flattery.

" They do possess such imitative grace,
    Such exquisite sympathy when needed most,
Such fine emotion feign'd with mobile face,
    Such passionate speech—withal the enormous boast,
The shallowness of hearts that seem so deep,
The candid lie that makes you laugh and weep.

" O grand traditions, forged me any morn,
    Ethereal sentiment for solid gold,
Vows soon unvow'd, oaths laughingly forsworn,
    Facts no historian happens to have told,
Fair, faint, false legends of a golden spring,
A past that never was a present thing.

" The thrush sings sweetest with his speckled breast
    Against the hawthorn jags, their poets say;
His loveliest notes are agony exprest,
    So that the little pain seems rapture : they,
So sharp, so soft, so pitiless, so forlorn,
Sing like the thrush, and stab ye like the thorn.

" God's pardon rest on them.   All that is o'er,
    The time of my departure is at hand,
And here my rest shall be for evermore,
    Far from Armagh and from that fatal land."
So he; yet still his frame was full of grace,
And death seem'd distant from that comely face,

Yet on All Saints, " Behold," the leeches said,
    " Before to-morrow must the Archbishop die ; "
Her loftiest rite the monastery made,
    And sang her music of festivity.
Thankless the task, inopportune the art,
To sing sweet songs to sorrow's heavy heart.

And sorrow was in that Cistercian home—
    Sorrow untuned the chant of choir and priest.
One only tasted of Christ's honeycomb,
    One only knew the fulness of the feast.
All Saints to Malachy was but the small
Dim vesper of his glorious festival.

"Lover and friend are darkness—light within.
    Love is eternal; and I love my Lord,
And love ye all; haply my love may win
    Somewhat from Thee, O Christ! whom I regard
Humanly pitying, for man's heart is Thine;
Divinely helping, being Thyself divine.

"Let me not fall into the bitter pain
    Of death eternal for any pains of death.
Let Christ's omnipotence manifested reign,
    Making omnipotent one who languisheth,
Whose thought and will and memory growing dim,
A trinity of misery, call to Him."

So, near the twilight was the veil withdrawn.
    Into a morn-red sea did his sail-sweep—
A sea not dim with twilight, flushed with dawn,
    If grey mists melt, if God's belovèd sleep,
Why search the sea mists when he sails no more?
Why weep for him whose weeping all is o'er?

Then, though all look'd to see the fair soul sail
    Into the mystery o'er life's furthest line,
The moment that it cross'd might none prevail
    To note for a memorial, or divine
The very moment on God's clock to tell
When all was over, and when all was well.

Only the Abbot softly said—" Behold,
  Life is a sea, whose waters ever swing ;
A wood, whose leaves like bells are ever toll'd.
  A tranquil God makes tranquil everything.
Here is no trembling leaf, no wrinkling wave,
But such serenity as sleepers have.

  " Sleep, brother, sleep, until the golden year ;
    Until thou sing, ' Let us arise and see
If the vine flourish—whether the grapes appear,
    If all the red buds gem the Passion tree ? '
Till on our hearts shall breathe a better day,
And chase the clouds of human things away."

  Ah ! never sorrow comes that comes alone.
    Deep calleth unto deep, and wave to wave ;
Saint calleth unto saint, and ere hath grown
    Grass on one sod, there is another grave.
The angels of one death-bed come again—
White clouds returning after God's own rain.

  And Girard died.   The funeral just o'er,
    The monks were gather'd.   Now, it happen'd so
That in the scroll which Bernard evermore
    His garden made eternally in blow,
Unto the place in order was he come—
 " *Nigra, O filiæ ! sed formosa sum.*"

  " Curtains of Solomon, tents of Kedar—such
    This body is—the tent which robs our sight
So that it sees not through the foldings much
    Of the uncircumscribèd plenitude of light."
Thus in the presence of these childlike men
He tells his sorrows sweetly o'er again.

By the bier tearless had stood Clairvaux's chief,
  Tearless the rite intoned in priestly vest,
And done despite unto the spirit of grief,
  Lest they, perchance, should say who knew not
    Christ,
"See, the pierced Hand dries not all tears that flow,
The wounded Heart is not for every woe."

"And shall they say thou knowest me no more,
  After this human flesh which we wear still,
Than I am known by light waves on the shore,
  Or breezes blowing round a sunny hill?
Ah! there be some who bid us mourners dwell
With Nature's sympathies, so shall it be well.

" Mystic condolences of morn and eve
  Shall touch the heartache tenderly away,
The rivers and the great woods interweave
  A consolation lips can never say;
And with the sighing of the summer sea,
Come cadences that chant, ' we pity thee.'

" It is not so; who truly mourn shall trace
  Something sardonic in that fixed regard,
The quiet sarcasm of a great cold face,
  Staring for ever on, terribly starr'd—
A silver depth of delicate despair,
  An uncompassionate silence everywhere.

"Ah! as we weep three voices bid us guess,
  Three contradictions cross above our dead;
Earth answers us ' perhaps,' and ' no,' and ' yes.'
  ' Perhaps,' by glad streams is conjecturèd;
Resurgent roses breathe faint ' yes '; but ' no '
Sighs o'er the undeceiving death-white snow.

" How speaks that pitiless power impersonal?
   ' I who stand stirless on the starlit tracts;
I who impalpably pervade the All;
   I who am white on the long cataracts;
I through æonian centuries who perform
Instinct of spring, or impulse of the storm;

   " ' I in the greenwood who at May-time move
      With straggling clouds of hyacinth dark blue;
Who neither laugh nor weep, nor hate nor love,
      Who sleep at once and work, both old and new—
Work with such myriad wheels that interlace,
Sleep with such splendid dreams upon my face;—

   " ' When thou hast ask'd me " Are my loved ones near ?
      Surely this golden silence doth contain
Them deathlessly; their dim eyes hold some tear
      Delicious, born not of the showers of pain"—
When thou hast question'd me at hush of eve,
What right hast thou to say that I deceive?

   " ' Perhaps they say, " I pardon thee that wrong;
      Nay, love thee more divinely for it all;"
Perhaps they strengthen thee when thou art strong,
      Perhaps they walk with thee when shadows fall.
But this is all I have for thee; the fair
Absolute certitude is other where.'

" But we will comfort us for him to-day
   Whom in that altar tomb of ours we hid.
  Faith's ' Yes ' shall rise although the sky be grey,
   Like a bird singing on a coffin-lid,
And like a rescuer victorious Hope
Wade far out in death's foam to catch the rope.

"Think'st thou of me bath'd in the sea of bliss?
    Art thou unmindful of me, holy mind?
Thou who of light has enter'd the abyss,
    Art thou with God's great splendour intertwined,
A chalice with His fulness fill'd too high
For wine-drops of earth's colour'd memory?

  "Then must I think of thee, my Girard, aye,
    As I might think upon some lucent tide;
As I might think of some fair summer day,
    Profuse of shadows on the mountain-side;
As I might think of the high snows far kenn'd,
A cold white splendid quiet without end?

  "Nay, that were life which truly liveth not,
    Life lower than our life, and not above.
Thou, thou art near to God in thy fair lot;
    Nearer to God is fuller of God's love—
Fuller of Him who looks on us to bless,
Who is impassible, not compassionless.

  "God's life is to have mercy and forgive;
    One spirit with Him, thou, my Girard, art;
Wherefore thro' that great life which thou dost live
    There is unsuffering sympathy in thy heart.
Thou carest, though no care can pass thy gate,
And passioning not art still compassionate.

  "O, that strange tide! what time the midnight came—
    Thy last. The darkness darkened not. It grew
Into a dawn for thee—a flush of flame,
    A midnight dawn, translucent through and through.
Dying he sings, or e'er his lips grow dumb,
'*Laudate in excelsis Dominum.*'

"Then with such look as erst I saw him cast
    In dear old days upon Sir Tescelin,
'Father,' he cried, 'my Father, oh, how vast
    Our glory to be sons !' and so pass'd in
To perfect climates—spring, and summer sun,
Autumn's exuberance, winter's rest in one."

Sweet was the last day when the Pontiff rode
    From Lyons to Clairvaux.   Upon the hill
The burning sunset had already glow'd.
    Superbly looks the retinue, and still
The Roman clergy and the courtly throng
Wait for the pageant and the perfect song.

They paused, but no procession went to meet
    The movement of the rainbow-colour'd wave ;
No carpet was there for the Pontiff's feet,
    No crowd of knights and dames, as in the nave
Of Rheims or Rouen ; and as on he fared
No herald bow'd to him, no trumpet blared.

Lo ! for the purple prelates, monks in serge ;
    For the gemm'd crucifix a cross of stone ;
For music dying on the vast dim verge
    Of the groin'd roof, a sweet low monotone,
Like the sea's sigh heard on a headland path—
Such mystic beauty the Church Latin hath.

Now it sounds grand, and solemnly it rolls.
    Like blind men hearing ocean, so hear we
Therein the adoration of all souls,
    Voices out of a vast eternity,
The wondrous sighs that soar while they complain,
The unperturbèd rapture, the sweet pain.

Now intervolving richly type with type,
    Reticulated sounds with sounds enlace—
The thoughts by summers long of prayers made ripe,
    Writ by some gentle Tacitus of grace.
Leaf shadows on them now, a bird-lilt chime—
Now a grand hammer-stroke of triple rhyme.

They sang; straight out those heartfelt praises broke,
    Like the old arrows kindling as they flew;
They speak the accent that their Master spoke,
    Seeing life's highest object clearly through
Earth's perturbations—like the calm higher star
Seen steadfast through the comet's hair of fire.

Each knight bethought him of the tender days,
    Of small hands lifted at his mother's knee;
Each priest felt purer with that burst of praise,
    Each bishop fell to praying for his see.
While knight and priest and bishop concert kept,
The Pontiff lifted up his voice, and wept.

" Out of the ground the evil weed shall spring,
    The pestilence shall spread o'er Christian lands;
Black shall the plague be, fell the blossoming—
    Behold, the self-convicted sophist stands,
Posing those principles, denying these,
Weaving himself into parentheses."

" The gold dust rub thou off the radiant moth,
    The death's head of the heresy show thou there;
From the fell skull tear thou the fine cerecloth,
    Lift up thy voice, O Bernard ! do not spare,
Though the swarms thicken round thee, though the fly
Of France shall hiss to that of Italy."

"What though Abelard promise new-born thought,
   And Arnold liberty—that word of fire ;
Speak thou calm truth from God's own treasure brought,
   The better freedom from our own desire ;
The Church's dogma lion-like in rest
Of strong repose that faces foemen best."

Time for collation, food of garden growth,
   The ripe fruit crush'd into the temperate cup ;
Then, silence made, proudly and gladly both
   The seneschal proclaimeth, standing up :
" Enough for each and all the brethren hope,
And one fair fish for our dread lord the Pope."

The sumptuous Roman in that stern hall miss'd
   The chased orfevery, the peacock's pride,
The heavy cup, the tint of amethyst ;
   And each to each around the table sigh'd,
"Well till the light of Burgundy wax dim
To hear a saint, but not to dine with him !"

But the Pope, wholly wrapp'd in Bernard, learn'd
   That love hath lore which makes it wondrous wise.
Still in the lamp of these saints' hearts have burn'd
   Time's clearest lights; they with their gentle eyes,
In the deep fold of God's pavilion hid,
Knew the world better than the worldlings did.

Then to the church.   No pictured forms were there.
   With the eternal golden headache cinct ;
No heaven of precious stones without soft air
   Or sunny distance sweetly indistinct.
" I love," said Bernard, "no such rigid sky ;
Our heaven is Christ, not lapis lazuli."

E

The Romans look'd for altar cloth's design,
    Fulgent as the Byzantine work, and stiff
With rough meandering of the golden line ;
    A miracle of colouring—as if
In charmèd looms the sunset clouds were trick'd,
And magic wrought the matchless acupict.

The Romans look'd for vestments to display,
    Radiant with all the colours of the morn,
Rich with pineapple, and pomegranate spray :
    But Bernard pray'd—" Let art again be born,
With beauty not this lower atmosphere's.
He paints Christ ill who paints Him not with tears."

Then after psalms and vespers all expect,
    The Pontiff bow'd and bade the Abbot speak.
He rose, his chestnut hair with thin grey fleck'd,
    A little flush upon his pallid cheek,
And oped the Song at that place of the lay
Which saith, " *Pascitur inter lilia.*"

Preluding something for the knights' behalf,
    Of virgin knights who keep a virgin will—
Serious, who almost deem it sin to laugh,
    Bearing the red cross upon Sion's hill ;
Who with strong arm corporeal possest
The place corporeal of our Jesus' rest,

He added—" Jesus, Lily for our eyes.
    Lo ! from the midst those spikelets all of gold,
Cinct with the white disposèd circlet-wise.
    Golden divinity in this behold,
With fair Humanity pure white around Him,
Christ with the crown wherewith his Mother crown'd Him.

" Lily and lilies, fair perfumèd towers,
    And all things that be His true lilies are—
His birth, His words, His works, His passion hours,
    His life risen beyond the morning star.
Joy to our sinful hearts from each is sent ;
For each is white, and each is redolent.

" Ah ! we are poor, and yet it shall be well
    If we can keep our narrow garden so
That He who feeds among the lilies dwell
    In hearts where we have made one lily grow—
So that each little life be turned by grace
Into one lily perfect in its place."

I closed both books ; the double spell was o'er.
    I slept, but a voice spake with gentle might,
" Open to me, open the long closèd door ;
    My locks are fillèd with the drops of night.
From some far shore, perchance across the sea,
Through drift and rain, O soul, I come to thee."

I saw a Hand, and raised my hands from thence—
    Were my hands wet with myrrh or tears so late ?
If there were myrrh, 'twas myrrh of penitence ;
    Of penitence that I had made him wait.
If there were tears, it was because I knew
That Hand of love was love-pierced through and through.

Then to the Frenchman's vaudeville I turn'd—
    There stands a law for every tongue of man,
They only can interpret who have learn'd ;
    To the unlearn'd it is barbarian.
Lay of the lily, dreamland of the dove !
Love hath a tongue they only know who love.

THE NEW ATLANTIS.

ARGUMENT.

I. Oxford in 1845—reading the *New Atlantis* of Bacon—II. Vision of the Island—III. Imaginatively applied to an idealized Oxford—IV. Oxford in 1885—Disappointment—Discord of Faith and Science in an age of Criticism—V. The inner work—the hope of reconciliation.

I.

A CITY of young life astir for fame,
    With generations each of three years' date,—
The waters fleeting, yet the fount the same—
    Where old age hardly enters thro' the gate.

Forty years since! Thoughts now long over-blown
    Had just begun to quicken in the germ.
We sat discussing subjects dimly known
    One pleasant evening of the Summer Term.

So question came of all things new and old,
    And how the Movement sped and where should lead?
Some, peradventure, scorn'd, but more wax'd bold,
    And bravely flaunted their triumphant creed.

Grave grew the talk, and golden grew the gloom;
  The reason might be weak, the voice was strong.
Outside, by fits and starts, from room to room,
  Boy call'd to boy, like birds, in bursts of song.

Of forms they talked that rose, as if in joy,
  Like magic isles from an enchanted foam;
They prophesied (no prophet like a boy!)
  Some fairer Oxford and some freer Rome,—

An Oxford of a more majestic growth—
  A Rome that sheds no blood, and makes no slave—
The perfect flower and quintessence of both,
  More reverent science, faith by far more brave.

Faith should have broader brow and bolder eye,
  Science sing "Angelus" at close of day;
Faith have more liberal and lucent sky,
  And science end by learning how to pray.

And "Hail the hour," they cried, "when each high morn
  England, at one, shall stand at the church gate,
And vesper bells o'er all the land be borne,
  And Newman mould the Church, and Gladstone
  stamp the State."

Now, when all left me, on my table lay
  A volume of my Bacon, where was writ
By that great hand, in the evening of his day,
  The fairest fable sunshine ever lit.

While in the dusk white chestnut blossoms paled
  Above the black old wall, on the great tree,
The book and talk commingled, and I sail'd
  Across a vast unnavigated sea.

II.

The enchanted island rose before me, drawn
   More beautiful than words of mine may reach;
It lay magnificent in a magic dawn,
   And full of boscage to the foam-fringed beach.

How well the city of the sons of knowledge
   Stood, giving pleasant prospect to the sea!
The fabulous and fancied island college
   Unfabled and unfancied grew for me.

In secret conclave of a sea so vast—
   Earth's widest wilderness of waves ring'd round—
No mariner ever caught from any mast
   A glimpse or inkling of that happy ground.

Yet now (such fair adventure did I win!)
   That I could see and hear whate'er of state
Or thought, or work, or worship, was within
   That muse-discovered island fortunate.

I saw the House of Solomon strongly stand,
   No fane so noble springs from any sod;
The oracle and lanthorn of the land,
   Where nature is the interpreter of God.

The College of the Six Days' Work well call'd,
   Whence traders issue—not for gain or might,
For gold or silk, for spice or emerald—
   Only for God's first creature, which is light.

I saw the masters of the speech and pen,
   Those cunning in the secret cause of things;
Whose aspect was as if they pitied men—
   A temperate race, a commonwealth of kings.

And, reverencing self, each soul was great,
  And, reverencing God, to each was brought
With long calm striving strength inviolate,
  With virgin purity victorious thought.

Being such they scorn the mob's vain fierce desires,
  Whereof coherent reading may not be,
Like the wild message interrupted wires
  Send in magnetic storms below the sea.

Deep caverns had they in the mountains wrought,
  High watch-towers for the clouds and starry tracts;
And many a spacious house where light was caught
  From tumbling tides and thunderous cataracts.

Gardens they had where they perused the flowers,
  And each had more than fairy tales to tell,
For with it bees that buzz'd in golden hours
  Conspired to work a patient miracle.

Exquisite distillations, dainty work
  Of excellent lustre, gems elsewhere unfound,
They lack'd not, nor the music that doth lurk
  In tremulous string and half inaudible sound.

The chemistry of sunlight and of star
  They knew; the long slow change of earth and man;
The bells and rings that sweet and dainty are—
  The universal calm æonian;

The families of all children of the cloud;
  The innumerable lives all waves that throng;
Each medicinal plant with pow'r endow'd;
  The birds of every wing and every song.

Pictures they had, silent and old, and yet
   Sweeter than music, richer-hued than rose,
And statues of their great men, stirless set,
   Praxitelean shapes in passionless repose.

A place of leafiness, a land of rivers,
   A clime where frosts in rain and sunshine pass,
And temperate nature, half-regretful, shivers
   The rose in heaven, the diamond on the grass.

A land of distant forests purple-domed,
   Of sunlit sails slow passing park-girt halls,
As sweet a land as traveller ever roam'd
   Through scented limes, by passioning waterfalls.

Yet deem'd I "Something wants where all is fair,"
   I sigh'd, "Man doth not live alone by bread"—
"What of the higher life, whose breath is prayer?
   What of the touch of sacraments?" I said.

Behold! a chime of bells rang toward the east,
   To a cathedral moved a white-robed host,
And of the wisest each man was a priest,
   And broadest brows were those that brighten'd most.

Within, i' the midst, was a scroll clasp'd with gold,
   And one stood forth of look more sweet than strong,
And (for the day was festival) he told
   "The Finding of the Book," in measured song.

"One eve like this, a thousand years ago,
   Our merchantmen of light were weary grown;
Wise men are strong, but for the strong 'tis woe
   To know the holiest of truth unknown.

" Lo ! through the trees, like bits intensely shining
    Cramp'd in the painted window, first there came,
Cut into diamonds by the boughs entwining
    The orange flashes of the sea aflame.

" And then through all the cloister'd aisles of beech,
    The fluted stems from whence the builder learns,
There pass'd a softer breath than any speech—
    A dying light stream'd inward on the ferns.

" Those trees stand waiting through the silent years,
    Expecting some one who doth never come ;
So sternly happy over human tears,
    To human words so eloquently dumb.

" They wait some song that winters never sing,
    Some summer blue that eye hath never seen,
The far-off foot-fall of some spell-bound spring,
    That lingers unimaginably green.

" But through them passed that eve a mystic breath,
    A hint from God to all their leaves was given,
Some inarticulate news of life and death,
    The anticipation of some gift from Heaven.

" And when the sun had sunk, and the night was
    Cloudy and calm ; some mile into the sea
Upon our eastern coast it came to pass
    A light unspeakable hover'd far a-lee.

" There sail'd a pillar from some shore unknown,
    Pillar with cross atop, and both of light ;
And all the ocean hush'd its stormy tone,
    And awe was on the azure infinite.

"The throng upon the strand made not a stir,
 But boats put forth to see the lights divine,
And the crews stood as in a theatre,
 Beholding this, as if a heavenly sign.

"And after prayer the wisest of our wise,
 Toward the pillar rowed with muffled oar,
Half fear'd that at one sound beneath the skies,
 The delicate dream might fade for evermore.

"When, as the boat drew near the light of God,
 The moon being partly hid by pearly bars,
Pillar and cross did cast themselves abroad
 Into a firmament of many stars.

"What ark was that?　How chanced it on the tide?
 No gallant ship upon the ocean rode,
No lights were lit the mariners to guide,
 On pencilled spars no sail was moon-besnow'd.

"Sole there remain'd that tiny cedar ark,
 Wherefrom there grew one small green branch of palm,
Which open'd, nothing but the Book they mark,
 Wherein is written every holy Psalm;

"And all the histories of the Hebrew years,
 And all the treasury of soul-complaints,
And all the dim magnificence of seers,
 And all the sighs and silences of saints.

"And all the visions by the Patmian shore,
 Cycle in cycle orbing manifold,
And all the hopes that make the sweet heav'n more
 Than a mere mist of amethyst and gold.

"And chief enshrined above earth's waves of strife,
   The unfathomable words that Jesus saith—
And all the loveliness of one white Life,
   And all the pathos of one perfect Death."

III.

On the next eve, beside our glorious river,
   Forth from the throng I walk'd among the trees,
The rustle of whose leaves keeps time for ever
   To holy bells of ancient colleges.

"I will do justice to this place," I cried,
   "Endow it with imaginative gleam,
And let its outward frame be glorified
   With something of the glory of my dream."

Whereon my Oxford rose with airy motion,
   Superbly touch'd by sunset's magic spell,
Most like the fabulous college girt with ocean
   Far beyond Cambalene and Tyrambel.

And I could see and hear what fortuned there,
   The forms and voices of a noble band,
In love and all sweet brotherhood walking fair,
   The thinkers and the workers hand in hand.

Not only those who know all lights and shadows,
   On waves of language as they rise and fall,
And live their life upon the Attic meadows
   Beneath the plane in worlds Platonical;

Or those who the fine tissue of the lyre
   Antique can follow through its difficult woof,
Or who can march with soul that doth not tire
   Through the long process of the perfect proof.

Eyes, too, were there, deep orbs whereto was given
   Another and a vaster world to win,
The passionless pathway of the stars of heav'n
   Without, the subtler universe within—

Histories that seem to have no steadfast end,
   By one majestic purpose bounden still,
As rushing cataracts hang at distance kenn'd
   One great white wonder from the purple hill—

The quiet chronicles of rocks and flowers,
   The mystery of life enwrapped in awe,
The interworking of dissimilar powers
   Where all is harmony, for all is law,

Through light's long tide and ocean's silver roll,
   From the pale primrose to the furthest star,
In all the harp of man's immortal soul
   No strife to desecrate, no string to jar.

Each after each, some house of light upsprings,
   A visible sign of knowledge larger grown,
Where cunning hands have heap'd up precious things,
   And cut thy vision, Verulam, in stone.

Oh, lamps too long unlit, now bravely burning—
   One true philosophy that lives and grows;
Oh, happy hand of reverential learning,
   That brushes snails from Faith's unfolding rose!

Nor shall want strain of verse superbly wrought,
  For aye sweet Poesy renews her youth,
Hangs songs like hawthorn from the sharpest thought,
  And daisies o'er the ploughshare track of Truth.

And aye let Science disenchant at will,
  And set her features free from passion's trace
A new enchantment waits upon her still,
  New lights of passion fall upon her face.

And aye as Poesy is said to die,
  Her resurrection comes.   She doth create
New heaven, new earth, an ampler sea and sky,
  A fairer Nature, and a nobler fate ;

For stealth of Science, poverty of Fact,
  Indemnifies herself in gold of song,
And claims her heritage in that blue tract
  Of land which lies beyond the reach of wrong.

And being divine, believeth the Divine,
  And being beautiful, creates the fair,
And always sees a further mountain line,
  And stands delighted on a starrier stair.

Last, as the evening light wax'd richly dim,
  Melodious voice of yearning unsufficed,
Uprose Magnificat, and holy hymn,
  And wisdom's strong heart fell asleep in Christ.

IV.

Years—forty years—have pass'd away since then,
  And boys who bent to manhood's earliest strife
Are in the silent land, or see as men
  Few diamond spray-drops on the mill-wheel life.

What high fulfilment hath thy vision found?
   What fair adventure hath thy fancy brought?
With what rich wreaths is thy Utopia crown'd?
   And what success hath fallen to thy thought?

The thinkers and the workers walk apart
   Upon the banks of Isis and of Cam.
The worker from the thing miscall'd his heart
   Casts forth like ice his morsell'd epigram.

The thinker owns of mere subjective worth
   His thought, and piles his doubts like flakes of snow,
And o'er a darken'd universe drivels forth
   His feeble and immeasurable " No."

And that sweet story.   Ah ! the Book enfolden
   Unstain'd and glorious by the branch of palm,
O'er it the shaft of light and cross more golden,
   Round it the sea's illimitable calm ;

Came it so gently within cedar barr'd,
   And floated it on waves so grandly lit,
And kept the angels such a watch and ward,
   And arch'd such tender azure over it,

That the white page should be so darkly blotted
   By the high treason of the sceptic's ink,
And the one story of a life unspotted
   Fall into four as certain critics think ?

That the sweet breath of miracle should die,
   Like the brief odour of the cedarn ark,
On earth's one truest page be branded—Lie !
   On its one chronicle of sunlight—Dark ?

And He whom we adore with bended head,
   What tints are these the mockers intermix?
The riddle of the years is poorly read,
   A contradiction loads the crucifix.

They call Him King. They mourn o'er His eclipse,
   And fill a cup of half-contemptuous wine,
Foam the froth'd rhetoric for the death-white lips,
   And ring the changes on the word " divine."

Divinely gentle—yet a sombre giant ;
   Divinely perfect—yet imperfect man :
Divinely calm—yet recklessly defiant ;
   Divinely true—yet half a charlatan.

They torture all the record of the Life,
   Give—what from France and Germany they get,
To Calvary carry a dissecting-knife,
   Parisian patchouli to Olivet.

They talk of critical battle-flags unfurl'd,
   Of the wing'd sweep of science high and grand—
And sometimes publish to a yawning world
   A book of patchwork learning second-hand.

Wing'd did they say ? but different wings uplift
   The little living ecstasy sunward borne,
And the brown-feather'd thief, with one poor gift—
   To stoop and twitter as it steals the corn.

Ah ! up the chapel-aisles, in rows more thin,
   The priests pass eastward, and the scholars come,
And half-sad faces wear Arouet's grin,
   And half the old Magnificats are dumb.

Hush'd be such strains of bitterness or hate ;
   A hidden faith doth Oxford strongly keep.
If less of blue the wave irradiate,
   A purer salt lies many a fathom deep.

Patience ! God's House of Light shall yet be built,
   In years unthought of, to some unknown song,
And from the fanes of Science shall her guilt
   Pass like a cloud. How long, O Lord, how long ?—

When Faith shall grow a man, and Thought a child,
   And that in us which thinks with that which feels
Shall everlastingly be reconciled,
   And that which questioneth with that which kneels.

And that true Book—the lovely dream is o'er
   Which saw it shelter'd well beneath the palm,
Sent by a saint from some mysterious shore,
   Its tiny frigate floating o'er a calm.

No vessel bore it to a sacred isle,
   No magic kept it from the salt sea-spray,
It had no perfect charm of Grecian style,
   No shaft of glory heralded its way.

Yet, peradventure, shall diviner seem
   The chronicle of a severer truth,
Than all the fabulous colouring of the dream
   That tinted it so richly in our youth.

And yet, for all the puzzle of the lines,
   All the discordant copies stain'd with age,
A more miraculous lore it intertwines,
   A grander Christ looks radiant from its page.

For all the stammering of those simple men,
A four-fold unity of truth they reach :
Drops as of light fall from their trembling pen,
And Christ speaks through them with a tenderer
speech.

And through all time our father's faith shall speed,
And the old utterance be sent abroad,
'And eastward chanted rise the changeless creed—
O Light from Light, O very God from God !

But for the New Atlantis—for the Church
Where faith and knowledge heart-united dwell—
I think it lies far-off beyond our search,
Enfolded by the Hills Delectable.

SUPER FLUMINA.

I.

I read again that wondrous song,
So strongly sweet and sweetly strong,
That ancient poem, whose music shivers
With a chime of rolling rivers
  Through the forest of the psalms—
Now it droppeth some golden bead,
Hebrew litany, or creed,
On its rosary of the reed :
  Now among the dark-green palms,
And through the harp-hung willows grey,
It yearneth its sweet self away.
And then the stream is fleck'd with froth,
And then the psalm is white with wrath,
And all the sorrow of the verse
Swells out majestic to a curse.
  "Blessèd be thou, Psalm !" I said,
  " Whether thy deep words be read
  Soft and low with bended head ;
Or whether chance at vesper-tide
  In some minster grand and grey,
By the organ glorified,
  Soft the *Süper Flumina*

Rustles by the wreathen pillar,
While the hush of eve grows stiller,
Till you seem to hear a river,
Willows tremble, harp-strings quiver,
And a beautiful regret
To the heavenly Sion set."
"And why," I thought, "must she be still,
The Muse, that with her hallow'd fire
   Those chosen shepherds did inspire
Of Bethlehem and of Horeb's hill;
   And now, in exile chants again,
   Not less divinely, such a strain,
   As he the son of Jesse play'd
   In Kedron's olive-hoary glade,
The glittering grief upon his brow?
In Christ's own church must she rest now,
   Fair, angel-fair, but frozen, like
A marble maid whose death-white fingers
Enclasp a harp, o'er which she lingers
   Stone-silent, but may never strike?"

II.

Musing thus a spirit bright
Stood by me that summer night:
   "Come where the river rolleth calm
   Of that Babylonian psalm;
Thou shalt learn, by me reveal'd,
Why those holy lips are seal'd."

III.

Then on a great Assyrian quay,
Fast by the town of Nineveh,
At noon of night, methought I stood
Where Tigris went with glimmering flood.

And walls were there all storied round
With old grim kings, enthroned, encrown'd.
Strange-visaged chief, and wingèd bull,
Pine-cone, and lotus wonderful.
Embark'd, I floated fast and far,
　　For I was bound to Babylon.
　　I saw the great blue lake of Wan,
And that green island Ahktamar.
　　I saw above the burning flat
　　The lone and snow-capp'd Ararat.
But ever spell-bound on I pass,
　　Sometimes hearing my shallop creep,
　　With its cool rustle, through the deep
Mesopotamian meadow grass.
And now (as when by moons of old,
Grandly with wrinkling silver roll'd,
It glimmer'd on through grove and lea,
　　For the starry eyes of Raphael
Journeying to Ecbatane)
The ancient Tigris floweth free,
　　Through orange-grove, and date-tree dell,
　　To pearl and rainbow-colour'd shell,
And coral of the Indian sea.
Take down the sail, and strike the mast,
Here is Euphrates old, at last.
Begirt with many a belt of palm,
Round fragrant garden-beds of balm,
(In one whereof old Chelcias' daughter
Went to walk down beside the water,
The lily both in heart and name,
Whose white leaf hath no blot of shame,)
Grandly the king of rivers greets
His Sheshach's hundred-gated streets.
　　Through the great town the river rolls,

Through it another river fleets,
   Whose awful waves are living souls.
High up, the gardens folded fair,
Rainbow'd round many a marble stair,
Hang gorgeous in the starlit air;
And trees droop down o'er spouted fountains,
   That once the hunter Mede saw set
Far off upon the purple mountains,
   Blossom'd with white and violet.
But o'er the sea of living souls,
   And o'er the garden, and the wave,
A muffled bell, methinketh tolls,
   " For thee, earth's chief ones stir the grave."
And rises to the stars a cry
Of triumph and of agony,
Far over all the ancient East—
" How hath the golden city ceased ! "
In shadow of his dim blue room,
High overhead in painted gloom,
Like sunset cloud-encompass'd, Bel
Sleeps golden in his oracle.
Falleth a voice of far-off Pæans
   Down where the lion banner droops :
" There is a sword on the Chaldeans ;
   Bel boweth down and Nebo stoops."
Ah ! I hear a sound of woe
By Euphrates come and go,
From the Lebanonian snow.
Rolling wave and sighing breeze
Wash'd through firs and cedar-trees—
And the chesnuts' plumes of white
Tossing in a fierce delight—
And a voice that calls and calls,
Through the algums, set like walls,

Purple round white waterfalls.
Deepening aye the voice increased,
   River near, and forest far,
Half like funeral, half like feast,
   " Fallen, O thou Morning Star ! "
And on by many a basalt column,
Euphrates sang most sad and solemn,
As if the prophet scroll below
His billows touch'd him with a woe ;
As if e'en now he felt the beat
Of those predestined Persian feet ;
   As if through all his sea-like plain,
Through all his moonlit roll he hears
A music of immortal tears—
   A sobbing as of gods in pain—
A prophecy of far-off years,
   When Babylon should become a heap,
   Sleeping a perpetual sleep,
   In the Lord's strong indignation,
   A wilderness, a desolation :
High gate buried, broad wall broken,
Deed undone, and dree unspoken,
Wise men silent, captains drunken,
Out of her the great voice sunken,
Sea dried up, and fountain shrunken.

IV.

'Tis starlight.　 In the fiery heat
No longer doth the landscape wink,
And flicker to the water's brink ;
It washes by high gates of brass,
   Between its mounds like mountain ridges,
   And white-stoled forms on fairy bridges,

Like boats on seas that cross and meet
With their sails moon-besilvered, pass.
  Gleams from the naphtha cressets fall
  By Esarhaddon's sun-bright hall.
The soldier rests him from the wars,
  Mylitta's girls their dances weave,
  The wise men in the lustrous eve
Watch the great weird Chaldean stars,
  Bells in blue Heaven's cathedral chime—
  Hands on the silver clock of Time—
  "What of the night? what of the night?"
  Read, ye astrologers, aright!

v.

Who are these sitting by the billows,
With their harps hung upon the willows?
For some among the captor throngs
Bid them sing one of Sion's songs.

VI.

"Golden hopes are faded like the sunset,
  Wan and wither'd like the morning moon,
Golden songs are silent on the mountains,
  Golden harps of Judah out of tune.
Ah! we cannot sing those songs divinest,
  For, O Sion! we remember Thee,
Ah! our hearts miss sorely in this valley,
  The wild beauty of the hill and sea.
If there must be music from the exiles,
  Set we words of battle to the harp,
Sweep it as the wild wind sweeps the forest,
  Let the curse rise high, and fall down sharp!"

VII.

What time on Judah's hills they trod,
  Science of song to them was given,
The harpers on the harps of God,
  The poets of the King of Heaven.
Mournful their strains, but through them still
The hope of their return is seen,
Like a sun-silver'd sail between
  Dark sea and darkly purple hill.
Strange race ! that reads for ever scrolls,
  With future glories pictured bright,
  As sunsets' golden pencils write
  Those slanting sentences of light,
When tree-tops dusk, on dark green boles.
By the broad pulses of this river,
Keeping one even time for ever,
  Since Amraphel was King of Shinar,
They long for Jordan's spray and shout,
And linkèd music long drawn out,
  Passioning with song diviner,
  From waterfall to waterfall.
O, for the line of long green meadows,
Waters whose gleams are silver shadows,
Whose glooms, where wood-hung hills rise higher,
Are darkness dash'd with silver fire,
And glens through which those waters come,
With many a crashing downward call,
With sweeping sound of battle pomp,
With blaring of the battle trump
And double of the battle drum.
And sometimes dawn-blush'd, as with twine
Of rosy flowers of Palestine,

And sometimes touch'd with Paschal moons,
And sometimes yellowing in the noons,
   But always gushing like the swell
Of shawms and cymbals raised to Him
Who dwells between the Cherubim,
   The Holy One of Israel.

VIII.

I saw the star-lights all depart,
   I heard a shiver thro' the leaf,
I heard the river moan and start
   As if rememb'ring that old grief
He had in Eden, when the swell
Of Gihon and of Hiddekel
Told him that earth's glory fell.
I saw the white moon fade and fade,
Until her silver flower was laid
   Dead on the morning's passionate heart
But ere the city was dislimn'd,
And ere the starlit stream was dimm'd,
And ere the exiles ceased to weep
Beside Euphrates' mighty sweep,
That spirit came to me and said:
" Seest thou, why sacred song is dead?
Faith sets those tunes of sorrow high,
Love gives that longing to each eye,
Hope pledges them the victory.
O exiles from a brighter home !
O weepers by.a wilder foam !
O poets to whom God has given
On earth the starry harps of Heaven !
When to the city far off kenn'd
With love like theirs your eye shall bend,

And Heaven look closer through the tear
As hills look nigh when rain is near ;
When by life's stream your faith shall sigh,
When ye shall look with hope as high,
For Christ's eternal victory ;
God's Church, as in the years of old,
    Shall chant, and her sweet voice returning
    Shall touch the eyes with happy yearning,
Shall teach the deep heart's harp of gold."

THE ISLAND CHURCH.*

Poor was the peasant, poor and heavy-hearted,
   Gone were his fields, his children, and his wife,
The kindly friends of other days departed,
   The fine lights faded from the hills of life.

Glad threads of speech, if rough, the labourers mingle
   By their own fires, where their own smoke-wreaths curl,
But Onni sat beside the stranger's ingle,
   And steeped in tears the scant bread of a churl.

The young have hope; but on his head was shaken
   The snow that summer sun shall never thaw,
Yet bless'd are they whom Heaven has undertaken
   To chasten and to teach from God's own law.

O bread of God! O fields for ever sunny!
   O fadeless flowers upon life's craggiest shelves!
O better substance, more enduring money,
   By grace laid up within our hearts themselves!

Midsummer Day! All night the child has folden
   Himself in expectation, heart and head,
Like bee in some rich flow'r-bell dusty golden,
   With long sleep pleasantly disquieted.

* The idea of this poem is taken from one by Runeberg, of which
I have only seen a literal French translation.

Midsummer Day!   All night the rivers going
  By heath and holm triumphantly have slid;
All night a soft and silver overflowing
  From joy expected bathed the sleeper's lid.

Midsummer Day!   At morn the maiden merry
  Dons her green kirtle; in the hawthorn lane
The farmer's boy beneath the rows of cherry
  Brings hampers full of flow'rs in the wane.

Midsummer Day!   The sad and wrinkled peasant
  Smiles as he stands erect upon the sod:
" In holy church to-day it will be pleasant
  To taste the liberty of the sons of God.'

Midsummer Day!   They smother up the altar
  With coronals, the brightest of the year;
The village choir have practised well the Psalter,
  The grand old hymns to Finland ever dear.

The feast of flowers!   The old priest has conn'd over
  A brand-new homily—joyful yet perplexed—
Redolent of garden bloom and meadow-clover;
  "Behold the lilies," is the good man's text.

The feast of flowers!   Sky, ocean, earth, seem turning
  All things to flowers.   Midsummer winds expire
In perfumed music through the roses, burning
  Like wreaths of red flame on the gilded wire.

Flowers in the churches!   Every birchen column
  Blushes like dawn, or gleams as when it snows;
Their sweet breath in the holy air is solemn,
  Like warbled music when it comes and goes.

Flowers on the window-sill, and in the chamber,
   Flowers round the great stem of the village tree,
And far away of infinite blue and amber
   The rose of heaven, the violet of the sea.

Speaks out the peasant Onni : " O my master !
   But for a little while let me away.
Hark, through the woodland walks is rising faster
   The voice of them that keep their holiday.

" All winter long, when the wild wind was grieving,
   Thou know'st I drudged for thee in wet and cold ;
All spring, when God's great sunshine was inweaving
   Through forest-leaves his thousand nets of gold,

" I work'd thy flax ; and still the bounding river
   Swept with his sound of trumpets through the glade,
But my poor ear was sicken'd with the shiver
   That the monotonous shuttle always made.

" Worse, worse than that ; for we our gathering festal
   Once in the twelvemonth only have down here,
But saints and angels, on the sea of crystal,
   Their feast of flowers keep round th' eternal year.

" And much I dread, lest, when my dear Lord call me,
   The chants of Heaven sound strange within my heart,
The low base influence of the earth enthral me,
   Till I forget how I may bear my part.

" Yea, worse than all, six months how long and dreary,
   This starving soul of mine is unsufficed
With that sweet invitation to the weary,
   The music of the promises of Christ.

"O master !—let me call thee, O, my brother !—
  I pray thee by all prayers thy heart may search,
I pray thee by the days when with thy mother
  Thou kept'st the feast, O let me go to church !"

But the churl pointed to the stream, where sombre
  A great white mist was creeping from the hill,
Dulling the splendid laughters without number
  That twinkled on the water by the mill,

And said with thick voice, eloquent of the flagon,
  "There lies thy way to church, thou preaching loon !
Go in that boat alone, I have no waggon—
  Perhaps thy prayers to church will bring thee soon."

And Onni heard speechless, and taking only
  The oar, full heavy for that wrinkled hand,
A weak adventurer in his vessel lonely,
  Pray'd inly, "God of ocean and of land !

"Sweetly and strongly at Thy will far-bringing
  All fins in waves, all plumes upon the breeze,
Beautiful birds to western forest winging,
  And whatso passeth through the paths of seas,

"Me, of more value, with my soul immortal,
  Mine infinite futurity, than they,
Me, a wing'd voyager to Thy starry portal,
  Lead, loving Father ! to Thy church to-day."

Wearily, wearily, drags the oar, and slowly,
  Like a man blinded by the snow athwart
His smarting eyelids, trails the boat, and wholly
  Lost in the fog, the rower loses heart.

And ding dong, ding dong, ding dong, in the distance,
  The church bells sounded over holt and hill.
He dropp'd his oars, and, weary of resistance,
  Let the strong river bear him at its will,

Until at last the bark's keel sharply grated
  Upon the white sand of a little isle;
Then ding dong, ding dong, to the man belated.
  The bells first clash'd, then ceased a little while.

White clung the colourless mist on the island forest,
  Unbeautifying its green depths and fells;
Sad were his thoughts, but just when grief was sorest,
  A silver music changed upon the bells.

Then the mist thinn'd; the lustrous sky, from off it
  Sweeping one cloud, left interspace of blue,
One isle of summer-light, one voiceless prophet
  Of sunny touches that make all things new;

And kenn'd beyond the furthest intervening
  Of dark green hall, and sombre colonnade,
The northern river far away was sheening
  Like the dark blue of some Damascan blade.

"Ah, in the church are psalms divinely tender"—
  Yet here is music too, not earthly born,
Dropp'd downward by the skylarks as they render
  Some air heard up beside the gates of morn.

And in the woodland depths, with restless shiver,
  From branch to branch the countless wild birds sing;
So the swift bow of a musician ever
  Flits with the melody from string to string.

" Ah, in the church the flowers are surely glorious,
   And the old pillars look full bright and brave ;
And the great organ, trembling yet victorious,
   Keeps quivering on like light upon the wave.

" And better still, the good Priest of Christ's merits
   Speaks to believing hearts, right glad yet awed,
And launches sinful yet forgiven spirits
   On that great deep, the promises of God ;—

" Whilst I, far off from church, like one in blindness
   Groping, lose sacrament and pastoral tone.
The Lord commandeth not His loving kindness,
   I am cast out from His pavilion."

Yet here are flowers, and light, and voices mystic—
   Were never such, since when, as Scripture tells,
The High Priest in the Holiest moved majestic
   With gems oraculous and with golden bells.

And here are pillared pines, like columns soaring,
   With branches tall that like triforiums are,
And a soft liturgy of winds adoring,
   With echoes from some temple-gate ajar.

And that no consecration may be wanted,
   One gently passes through the haunted place—
Not like Him on the crucifixes painted,
   With white, cold, agèd, agonizing face—

Not crown'd with thorns, and ever bleeding, bleeding,
   Stains on that rigid form more dark than wine—
Not dead but living, beautiful exceeding,
   Divinely Human, Humanly Divine.

And Onni prays the prayer that knows no measure
　By bead, or clock, or count of regular chime—
The prayer which is the fulness of all pleasure,
　In words unutter'd, and transcending time.

His worship ended, Nature sang no longer,
　But grown contemplative was silent too;
And now made gladder, calmer, holier, stronger,
　He raised his voice, and bade his soft adieu.

"O, fellow-worshippers with me and Nature,
　Who sang God's praises with my soul forlorn,
Wild flower, and forest tree, and wingèd creature,
　And all the sunny sanctities of morn,

" River, whom God hath taught to be my pilot,
　Needles of light that dart through larch and birch,
Ripples that were the music of mine islet,
　And pines that were the pillars of my church—

"Peace, and Farewell."　Then happier and faster
　He glided homeward down the watery way,
And with a gentle smile, said, "Thank you, Master,
　" I was at church, I kept my feast to-day."

MUSIC OR WORDS?

(ON THE SEVEN LAST WORDS.)

AND is it well what one hath said ?—
" Ye who shall watch beside my bed,
Get music, not so much to swell
As to be half inaudible,
Around my agony.   While ye wait
My passing through the shadowy gate,
Speak me no word articulate.

" Touch for me, touch some tremulous chords—
Touch,—I am weary of all words—
Of hearing, be it e'er so sweet,
What hath capacity of deceit.
Let then my spirit on life's brink,
Some undeceiving music drink—
And so it shall be well, I think.

" Speak me no words—the poet sings
That all our human words have wings.
Ah ! if those wings at times attain
A golden splash on their dark grain
From some blue sky-cleft far away,
They mostly wear the black or grey
That doth beseem the bird of prey.

"Speak then no words—but some soft air
Play; as it scarcely ripples there,
Or, rather say, as its true wing
With silver over-shadowing
Throbs—and no more—my soul beneath
Shall pass without one troubled breath
From sleep to dreams, from dreams to death.

" Wherefore be utter'd words kept far,
Such as may that dim music mar,
—That exquisite vagueness finely brought,
A gentle anodyne to thought—
Speak me not any words, O friend !
At least one moment at life's end
I want to feel, not comprehend."

II.

How many words since speech began
Have issued from the lips of man ?
How few with an undying chant,
The gallery of our spirits haunt—
And with immortal meanings twined
More precious welcome ever find
From the deep heart of human-kind ?

Words that ring on world without end,
Words that all woe and triumph blend,
—Broken, yet fragments where we scan
Mirror'd the perfect God and man—
Words whereunto we deem that even
All power because all truth is given—
We. Christians only know of seven.

Three hours of an unfathom'd pain,
Of drops falling like summer rain,
Earth's sympathy and heaven's eclipse—
Three hours the pale and dying lips
By their mysterious silence teach
Things far more beautiful than speech
In depth or height can ever reach.

O kingly silence of our Lord!
O wordless wonder of the Word!
O hush, that while all heaven is awed,
Makes music in the ear of God !
Silence—yet with a sevenfold stroke
Seven times a wondrous bell there broke
Upon the cross, when Jesus spoke.

One word, one priestly word He saith—
The advocacy of the death,
The mediation by the Throne
Wordless beginneth with that tone.
All the long music of the plea
That ever intercedes for me
Is set upon the self-same key.

One saving word—though love prevails
To hold Him faster than the nails,
And though the dying lips are white,
As foam seen through a dusky night :
That hand doth Paradise unbar,
Those white lips tell of a world afar,
Where perfect absolutions are.

One word, one human word—we lift
Our adoration for the gift

Which proves that, dying, well He knew
Our very nature through and through.
Silver the Lord hath not nor gold,
Yet His great legacy behold—
The Virgin to the virgin-soul'd.

One word, the *Eli* twice wailed o'er—
'Tis anguish, but 'tis something more.
Mysteriously the whole world's sin,
His and not His, is blended in.
It is a broken heart whose prayer
Crieth as from an altar-stair
To One who is, and is not, there.

One word, one gentle word.   In pain
He condescendeth to complain—
Burning, from whose sweet will are born
The dewinesses of the morn.
The fountain which is last and first,
The fountain whence life's river burst,
The fountain waileth out, " I thirst."

One royal word of glorious thought.
A hundred threads are interwrought
In it—the thirty years and three,
The bitter travail of the Tree,
Are finished—finished too we scan
All types and prophecies—the plan
Of the long history of man.

One word, one happy word—we note
The clouds over Calvary float
In distances, till fleck or spot
In the immaculate sky is not;

But on the cross peace falls like balm,
And the Lord's soul is yet more calm
Than the *commendo* of His psalm.

III.

Word of the Priest, the one forgiver,
Word of the atonement wrought for ever,
Of Him who bore in depths unknown
The burden that was not His own—
Word of the human son and friend
That doth true human love commend
Until humanity shall end—

Word that bestow'd in one brief breath
The double gift of life and death—
Death to the sufferer sweet surprise,
Life in the lawns of Paradise—
Word in the passion-palm once writ,
And lo ! earth's waters all are lit
Now with pathetic touch of it—

Word that breathes forth for aye sithence
Record of more than innocence,
The full assurance reach'd at length,
The laying hold upon a strength—
The resignation sweet and grand
Of self into a Father's hand.
Quietly passing from this land—

Be more to me, at last, O words,
Than all that trembles from the chords !

Words that have no deceit or hate,
Be with me dying—I can wait,
If ye be with me on that day,
If your sweet strength within me stay,
A little for the harps to play.

THE OLD MAN AND THE SHIP.

AN ARMENIAN LEGEND.

"'Tis sunset, and the wind is blowing fair ;
    Her anchor soon the good ship will be weighing,
Toward the cross above the harbour stair
    The mariners are praying.

The sky was flaming westward, and the flood
    Was flashing all afire by bay and cape,
Till their dazed eyes upon the awful rood
    Could scarce discern the shape.

That all day long they saw from off the ship—
    The imaged Man of Sorrows on the Tree,
With blood drop on the brow, and thin white lip
    Above the pitiless sea.

Now they averr'd that some resplendence came
    And on the carven hair and face did smite,
Till in a furnace as of silver flame
    The whole was lost in light.

And in the glory as it disappear'd
    Suddenly hung an agèd Pilgrim there ;
White as the snow was his majestic beard,
    White as the snow his hair.

No thorny crown was on his ample brow,
　　No blood-drops issuing from side or palm,
Divinely was the bitter passion now
　　　Changed into passionless calm.

The fierce light faded then above, below,
　　And on the deck the sailors were aware
Of an old man, with beard as white as snow.
　　　Sweet was his pleading prayer :

"The land I seek is very far away—
　　Long have I tarried on this shore remote—
My brothers, ye are bound for it to-day,
　　　Oh, take me in your boat !

"So shall I sooner see its mountain line,
　　Its immemorial forests' purple dome,
And hear the musical murmurings divine
　　　Of rivers round my home.

"Those rivers run in crystal ever clearer,
　　Baptizing bluer violets on the sod,
And those eternal mountain-tops are nearer
　　　Than other hills to God.

"Silver and gold for guerdon have I none,
　　But prayers, deep prayers, I offer for my freight,
Such as Heaven's gentle heart have often won,
　　　When man hath said 'Too late !'"

The mariners replied, "Our ship is large
　　And words are light, and merchants must be paid ;
A ship like this, with all her heavy charge,
　　　Is not for prayers," they said.

Then stepp'd the old man down upon the sand,
  Wind-sifted, sparkling as the mountain sleet,
And scoop'd it with his thin and feeble hand,
    And flung it at his feet.

And down it fell in spangles on the shore,
  A marvellous dust of silver and of gold,
Nor ceased until the mariners twice o'er
    The grey-beard's freight had told.

Blind souls of men refusing their true bliss,
  God's highest offers, and yet sweetly still
He bribes them by these lower gifts of His,
    Against their own proud will !

So to the bark once more the pilgrim pass'd.
  Out sail'd the gallant vessel homeward bound,
But evermore in silence by the mast
    The pilgrim might be found.

While the ship raced upon an even keel
  And floated buoyant as an ocean bird,
Upon the deck, or up beside the wheel,
    No voice of his was heard.

Only sweet virtues grew beneath his eye—
  Both Charity and Hope, which are Heaven's sole
Prime roses, and Humility, the shy
    Meek violet of the soul.

Only at vesper-tide, from time to time,
  Invisible angels, from the starlit stair,
Touch'd all their spirits to a more sublime
    And an intenser prayer.

Only by night, what time they cross'd the pale
   Moonlight into the darkness, high and higher
Each topmast seem'd a cross, and its white sail
     Was snow'd with sacred fire.

At last a storm rush'd down upon the flood,
   And the tyrannic winds sang loud and strong;
The pilot cried, "Beneath this dreadful scud
     No vessel can live long."

Soon rose surmise who might the pilgrim be,
   His passage money how he came to win;
"God's wrath," they thought, "is working in the sea
     Because of this man's sin."

Whereat the old man rose, and, "Through the storm
   Give me your ship," he said, and straight did take
Mysterious likeness to the wondrous Form
     On Galilee's wild lake.

"Sleep sweetly while the ocean works and stirs,
   Sleep sweetly till we cross the seething bar,
Sleep on, and take your rest, O mariners,
     For mine own crew ye are."

So look'd He upward with his calm bright eye,
   So made the holy sign with His right hand,
His left upon the helm—immediately
     The ship was at the land.

But as the ship with all sail set was steer'd
   Bravely into the port around the cape,
No more might ye have seen a silver beard,
     No more an old man's shape.

But calm He stood, as when He wears His crown
    Upon the Calvary on some southern peak,
Or where above the altar He looks down,
    With blood-drops on His cheek.

And those who knew the Cross so far away,
    Toward which they pray'd above the harbour stair,
Said that its perfected reflection lay
    Upon the Pilgrim there.

So the shore redden'd with the holy dawn,
    And the bells chimed from all the churches round,
And the long surf's fall on the beach was drawn
    Into one psalm-like sound.

And, "Rise from your sweet sleep," the hymn outrang,
    "From your sad dream, or from your slumber sweet:
Here is our Lord, and here our ship," they sang,
    "Oh, fall at Jesus' feet!"

VENICE, 1872.

[This legend is given in a small collection which I read in the Armenian Convent.]

REPENTANCE AND FAITH.

THERE was a ship, one eve autumnal, onward
    Steer'd o'er an ocean lake;
Steer'd by some strong hand ever as if sunward;
    Behind, an angry wake,
Before there stretch'd a sea that grew intenser
    With silver fire far spread
Up to a hill mist-gloried, like a censer
    With smoke encompassèd:
It seem'd as if two seas were brink to brink,
A silver flood beyond a lake of ink.

There was a soul that eve autumnal sailing
    Beyond the earth's dark bars,
Toward the land of sunsets never paling,
    Toward Heaven's sea of stars;
Behind there was a wake of billows tossing,
    Before, a glory lay.
O happy soul! with all sail set just crossing
    Into the Far away,
The gloom and gleam, the calmness and the strife,
Were death behind thee, and before thee life.

And as that ship went up the waters stately,
  Upon her topmasts tall
I saw two sails, whereof the one was greatly
  Dark as a funeral pall.
But oh, the next's pure whiteness who shall utter?
  Like a shell-snowy strand,
Or when a sunbeam falleth through the shutter
  On a dead baby's hand ;
But both alike across the surging sea
Help'd to the haven where the bark would be.

And as that soul went onward, sweetly speeding
  Unto its home and light,
Repentance made it sorrowful exceeding,
  Faith made it wondrous bright ;
Repentance dark with shadowy recollections,
  And longings unsufficed,
Faith white and pure with sunniest affections
  Full from the Face of Christ.
But both across the sun-besilver'd tide
Help'd to the heaven where the heart would ride.

YOUTH RENEWED.

Yes; with heavy dashing
  Of a shower just shed,
On the gloomy beech tree,
  Wet were leaves o'erhead.
Wet were all the roses
  On the garden wire,
Wet were all the corn-fields,
  Flakes of yellow fire.

By the gloomy beech tree,
  By the roses wan,
Looking on the corn-fields,
  Whence the gold was gone,
Walked I sadly thinking,
  " I am no more young,"
When among the dripping
  Leaves a wild bird sung.

Ah ! I thought, it chanted
  Some immortal strain
Of a silver sunshine
  Coming after rain ;

Of a richer flushing
  On a finer rose ;
Of a tint more golden
  Than the autumn knows.

Yes ; with sorrow wetted
  In life's autumn day,
Is the cheek full often
  When the hair grows grey ;
All the leaves and blossoms
  Drip with rain of tears,
And the sheaves lie sodden
  On the field of years.

Then a sweet bird singeth
  Of a joy that lies
In the grief that only
  Maketh love more wise ;
Sings of youth more happy,
  Sunlight more divine—
Gentle bird, sweet Spirit,
  What a song is thine !

Forty seems as old age
  In youth's happy light.
Fifty counts as nonage
  When the head is white.
Fifty, sixty, seventy—
  Old age cometh never,
If the life gives the life
  Which is for ever and ever.

I.

A SEA GLEAM.

'TWAS a sullen summer day;
　Skies were neither dark nor clear,
　Heaven in the distance sheer
Over sharp cliffs sloped away—
　Ocean did not yet appear.

Not as yet a white sail shimmer'd,
　Not with full expanse divine
　Did the great Atlantic shine;
Only very far there glimmer'd
　Dimly one long tremulous line.

In the hedge were roses snow'd
　Or blush'd o'er by summer morn,
　Right and left grew fields of corn,
Stretching greenly from the road—
　From the hay a breath was borne.

Not of small sweet wild rose twine,
　Not of young corn waving free,
　Not of clover fields thought we;
Only to that dim bright line
　Looking, cried we, "'Tis the sea."

H

In life's sullen summer day
　　Lo ! before us dull hills rise,
　　And above, unlovely skies,
Slope off with their bluish grey
　　Into some far mysteries.

Love's sweet roses, hope's young corn,
　　Green fields whisper'd round and round
　　By the breezes landward bound
(Yet, ah ! scalded too and torn
　　By the sea winds), there are found.

And at times in life's dull day,
　　From the flower, and the sod,
　　And the hill our feet have trod
To a brightness far away,
　　Turn we saying, " This is God."

II.

AMONG THE SAND-HILLS.

From the ocean half a rood
　　To the sand-hills long and low
　　Ever and anon I go ;
Hide from me the gleaming flood,
　　Only listen to its flow.

HINTS OF THE DIVINE.

To those billowy curls of sand
  Little of delight is lent—
  As it were a yellow tent,
Here and there by some wild hand ·
  Pitch'd, and overgrown with bent.

Some few buds like golden beads
  Cut in stars on leaves that shine
  Greenly, and a fragrance fine
Of the ocean's delicate weeds,
  Of his fresh and foamy wine.

But the place is music haunted.
  Let there blow what wind soever ;—
  Now as by a stately river,
A monotonous requiem's chanted ;
  Now you hear great pine woods shiver.

Frequent when the tides are low
  Creep for hours sweet sleepy hums.
  But when in the spring tide comes,
Then the silver trumpets blow
  And the waters beat like drums.

And the Atlantic's roll full often,
  Muffled by the sand-hills round,
  Seems a mighty city's sound,
Which the night-wind serves to soften
  By the waker's pillow drown'd :

Seems a salvo—state or battles—
  Through the purple mountain gaps
  Heard by peasants ; or perhaps
Seems a wheel that rolls or rattles ;
  Seems an eagle's wing that flaps ;

Seems a peal of thunder, caught
  By the mountain pines and tuned
  To a marvellous gentle sound ;
Wailings where despair is not,—
  Hearts self-hushing some heart wound.

Still what winds there blow soever,
  Wet or shine, by sun or star,
  When white horses plunge afar,
When the palsied froth-lines shiver,
  When the waters quiet are ;

On the sand-hills where waves boom,
  Or with ripples scarce at all
  Tumble not so much as crawl,
Ever do we know of whom
  Cometh up the rise and fall.

Need is none to see the ships,
  None to mark the mid-sea jet
  Softening into violet,
While those old pre-Adamite lips
  To those boundary heaps are set.

Ah ! we see not the great foam
  That beyond us strangely rolls,
  Whose white-wingèd ships are souls
Sailing from the port called Home,
  When the signal bell, Death, tolls.

And we catch not the broad shimmer,
  Catch not yet the hue divine,
  Of the purpling hyaline ;
Of the heaving and the glimmer
  Life's sands cheat our straining eyne.

But by wondrous sounds not shut
  From those sand-hills, we may be
  Sure that a diviner sea
Than earth's keels have ever cut
  Floweth from eternity.

HIS NAME.

O WONDERFUL! round whose birth hour
Prophetic song, miraculous power,
Cluster and burn, like star and flower.

Those marvellous rays that at Thy will,
From the closed Heaven which is so still,
So passionless, stream'd round Thee still,

Are but as broken lights that start,
O Light of Light, from Thy deep heart;
Thyself, Thyself, the wonder art!

O Counsellor! four thousand years,
One question tremulous with tears,
One awful question vex'd our peers.

They asked the vault—but no one spoke;
They asked the depth—no answer woke;
They ask'd their hearts that only broke.

They look'd, and sometimes on the height
Far off they saw a haze of white,
That was a storm, but look'd like light.

The secret of the years is read,
The enigma of the quick and dead,
By the Child voice interpreted.

O everlasting Father, God !
Sun after sun went down, and trod
Race after race the green earth's sod,

Till generations seem'd to be
But dead waves of an endless sea,
But dead leaves of a deathless tree.

But Thou hast come, and now we know
Each wave hath an eternal flow,
Each leaf a lifetime after snow

O Prince of Peace ! crown'd and discrown'd,
They say no war nor battle's sound
Was heard the tired world around.

They say the hour that Thou did'st come,
The trumpet's voice was stricken dumb,
And no one beat the battle-drum.

Yea, still as life to them that mark
Its poor adventure, seems a bark
Whose track is pale, whose sail is dark :

Thou, who art Wonderful, dost fling
One ray, till, like the sea-bird's wing,
The canvas is a snowy thing—

Till the dark boat is turn'd to gold,
And all the great green ocean roll'd
With anthems that are new and old,

With noble path of luminous ray
From the boat slanting all the way
To the Island of undying day.

And still as clouding questions swarm
Around our hearts, and dimly form
Their problems of the mist and storm :

As fleeting years seem poorly fraught
With broken words, wherefrom is wrought
Nathless of love the loveliest thought,

Mere meaningless syllables chance met,
Though in one perfect poem yet
Uninterrupted to be set ;

And when not yet in God's sunshine,
The smoke drifts from the embattled line
And shows the Captain's full design ;

We bid our doubts and passions cease,
Our restless fears be still'd with these—
Counsellor, Father, Prince of Peace !

VERY FAR AWAY.

ONE touch there is of magic white,
  Surpassing southern mountain's snow,
That to far sails the dying light
  Lends, where the dark ships onward go
Upon the golden highway broad
That leads up to the isles of God.

One touch of light more magic yet,
  Of rarer snow 'neath moon or star,
Where, with her graceful sails all set,
  Some happy vessel seen afar,
As if in an enchanted sleep
Steers o'er the tremulous stretching deep.

O ship! O sail! far must ye be
  Ere gleams like that upon ye light.
O'er golden spaces of the sea,
  From mysteries of the lucent night,
Such touch comes never to the boat
  Wherein across the waves we float.

O gleams more magic and divine,
　Life's whitest sail ye still refuse,
And flying on before us shine
　Upon some distant bark ye choose.
—By night or day, across the spray,
That sail is very far away.

THE BIRTHDAY CROWN.

IF aught of simple song have power to touch
Your silent being, O ye country flowers,
    Twisted by tender hands
      Into a royal brede,

O hawthorn, tear thou not the soft white brow
Of the small queen upon her rustic throne,
    But breathe thy finest scent
      Of almond round about.

And thou, laburnum, and what other hue
Tinct deeper gives variety of gold,
    Inwoven lily, and vetch
      Bedropp'd with summer's blood,

I charge you wither not this long June day !
Oh, wither not until the sunset come,
    Until the sunset's shaft
      Slope through the chestnut-tree ;

Until she sit, high-gloried round about
With the great light above her mimic court—
    Her threads of sunny hair
      Girt sunnily by you.

What other crown that queen may wear one day,
What drops may touch her forehead not of balm,
What thorns, what cruel thorns,
I will not guess to-day.

Only, before she is discrowned of you,
Ye dying flowers, and thou, O dying light,
My prayer shall rise—" O Christ !
Give her the unfading crown.

" The crown of blossoms worn by happy bride,
The thorny crown o'er pale and dying lips,
I dare not choose for her—
Give her the unfading crown !"

CHRIST ON THE SHORE.

In the silence of the morning,
  Of the morning grey and clouded,
    Mist enshrouded,
  On the shore of Galilee,
Like a shape upon a column,
    Sad and solemn
  Christ is standing by the sea,
In the silence of the morning.

On the waters cold and misty,
  Like a rock, its dark back lifting
    Through the drifting
  Vapours, heaves the fisher's boat.
Still through grey-fog hood and mantle
    That most gentle
  Watcher looketh where they float
On the waters cold and misty.

Hearts are waiting, eyes are weeping,
  Comes a voice, a susurration ;
    Tribulation
  Melteth, melteth like the mist ;

Yet, like music rich and olden
        Hiding golden
Words, that sweet voice hideth Christ
From the hearts that wait, and weep Him.

In another morning silence,
    When a greyer fog falls dreary
        And we weary
    With the sea's beat evermore,
Cometh One, and pale and wounded,
        Mist-surrounded,
    Looketh from another shore
In another morning silence.

Other waters cold and misty
    On the wet sands grandly singing,
        Bear a swinging
    Little bark call'd Life by men;
While the bark is swinging slowly,
        That most Holy
    Watcher looks: light silvers then
On the waters cold and misty.

Hearts are waiting, eyes are weeping,
    Falls a voice, O sweet but broken!
        Falls a token
    Light bedimm'd with blinding mist.
Take us where there are no ocean's
        Wild commotions;
    Where we shall not know, O Christ!
Weary hearts, or tear-wet eyelids.

THE CHAMBER PEACE.

A SUMMER night that blows,
Fragrant with hay and flowers, on copse and lawn—
A window muffled round and round with rose,
    Fronting the flush of dawn.

O pilgrim, well is thee
Till the day break, and till the shadows cease,
Resting the faint heart and the failing knee,
    In that sweet chamber, Peace.

The white moon through the trees
Sails—but thou singest to a heavenly tune,
" Needeth no sun the land my spirit sees,
    " Neither by night the moon."

Before thine eyes half closing
Like ink-black plumes their tops the willows shake ;
Through them thou seest a little boat reposing
    Upon a moonlit lake,

And " O," thou say'st, " my soul
Was like those inky plumes the night winds toss ;
But now it hangs in one great silver roll
    Over a hidden Cross.

Ever on life's wild swell
My heart went drifting, drifting on remote,
But now within the veil 'tis anchor'd well,
Safe as that little boat."

Or if the shower that lingers
In fleecy clouds of moonlight-tissued woof
Falls, and the soft rain with a hundred fingers
Taps on the chamber roof,—

" Christ," the lone pilgrim saith,
" My Saviour, comes this heart's poor love to win ;
Thy locks are fill'd with dew," he murmureth,
" Oh that Thou wouldst come in."

So rests the pilgrim ever,
Hearing at solemn intervals a swell,
Music as of a grandly falling river
On Hills Delectable.

So rests he till he knows
The morning redden in the eastern skies,
And fronts the unfolding of heaven's fiery rose,
The beautiful sunrise.

Another chamber yet—
The curtain is of grass, and closely drawn ;
But the pale pilgrim, in its portal set,
Looketh toward the dawn.

Ofttimes red roses lie
On the green curtain of that chamber low,
And blossoms like the deep blue summer sky,
Or like the winter snow.

And when the eves are calmest,
Up in the incense-laden aisles of lime,
Some sweet bird meditateth like a psalmist
His poesy sublime.

So lay the pilgrim down—
Set thou his feet, and face, and closèd eyes,
Where they may meet the golden raying crown
Of Christ's august sunrise.

So let him rest, unheard
Thy faithless mourning ; let thy murmur cease ;
Translate the grave into a gentler word,
Call it the " Chamber Peace."

A FINE DAY IN HOLY WEEK.

THERE is a rapturous movement, a green growing
 Among the hills and valleys once again,
And silent rivers of delight are flowing
 Into the hearts of men.

There is a purple weaving on the heather,
 Night drops down starry gold upon the furze,
Wild rivers and wild birds sing songs together,
 Dead nature breathes and stirs.

Is this the season when our hearts should follow
 The Man of Sorrows to the hills of scorn ?
Must not our pilgrim grief be scant and hollow
 On such a sunny morn ?

Will not the silver trumpet of the river
 Wind us to gladsomeness against our will ?
The subtle eloquence of sunlight shiver
 What sadness haunts us still ?

If I might choose these notes should all be duller,
 That silver trump should fail in Passion week ;
The mountain-crowning sky wear one pale colour,
 Pale as my Saviour's cheek.

And day and night there should be one slow raining,
  With mournful plash, upon the moor and moss,
And on the hill one tree, its bare arms straining ;
    Bare as my Saviour's cross.

Nay, if thy heart were sorrowful exceeding,
  Its pulses big with that divinest woe,
These natural things would only set it bleeding
    To think it should be so—

To think that guilty and degraded Nature
  Could look as joyful as she looketh now,
When the warm blood has dropp'd from her Creator
    Upon her branded brow.

A FINE DAY ON LOUGH SWILLY.

Soft slept the beautiful autumn
  In the heart, on the face of the Lough—
  Its heart, whose pulses were hush'd,
Till you knew the life of the tide
But by a wash on the shore.
A whisper like whispering leaves
  In green abysses of forest—
  Its face, whose violet melted,
    Melted in roseate gold—
  Roses and violets dying
  Into a tender mystery
    Of soft impalpable haze.

Calm lay the woodlands of Fahan :
The summer was gone, yet it lay
On the gently yellowing leaves
  Like a beautiful poem, whose tones
  Are mute, whose words are forgot,
  But its music sleepeth for ever
  Within the music of thought.
  The robin sang from the ash,
  The sunset's pencils of gold

No longer wrote their great lines
On the boles of the odorous limes,
Or bathed the tree-tops in glory,
But a soft strange radiance there hung
In splinters of tenderest light.
And those who look'd from Glengollen
Saw the purple wall of the Scalp,
As if through an old church window
Stain'd with a marvellous blue.

From the snow-white shell strand of Inch
You could not behold the white horses
Lifting their glittering backs,
Tossing their manes on Dunree,
And the battle boom of Macammish
Was lull'd in the delicate air.
As in old pictures the smoke
Goes up from Abraham's pyre,
So the smoke went up from Rathmullen ;
And beyond the trail of the smoke
Was a great deep fiery abyss
Of molten gold in the sky,
And it set a far track up the waters
Ablaze with gold like its own.
Over the fire of the sea,
Over the chasm in the sky,
My spirit as by a bridge
Of wonder went wandering on,
And lost its way in the heaven.

The ship is out on the lake,
The fisherman stands on the deck.
Rosy and violet sea ;
Delicate haze in the distance ;

> Woodlands softer than summers ;
> Great golden eye of intense,
> Concentrated marvellous light ;
> Mysterious suggestions of thought ;
> Beautiful yearnings of fancy ;
> Wonderful imaginations ;
> Throbs of the being immortal
> Who, prison'd deep in the heart,
> Looks through the bars of the flesh :—
What recketh he of them all ?
So to the reasonless eye
> The Master's picture is only
> A heap of colouring flat,
> A strange confusion of strokes,
> And thought, and study, and books,
> And fine traditions of taste,
> Are the glasses through which we survey
> The beauty of natural things,
> Till stars come splendidly out
> That our eyes would have never beheld ;
> And cultured association
> Hangeth to things that we see,
> Hints and prophetical types,
Shadows grand and immortal,
Sacraments dim and delightful,
Of the things that the eye hath not seen.

O this ship and ocean of life !—
I, like the fisherman's boy,
> On this awful beautiful sea
> Gaze on a glory for ever
That I love not, nor know as I ought—
> Sail on a beautiful deep,
> Hear the soft washing of waves

That set to the shore of our God—
Look on purpureal hills,
Look on exquisite woods,
   Soft, and most solemn and stately—
Sail toward the gate of Heaven,
   Yet know it not, nor consider!

Hues more radiant by far
Than the Autumn ever could give
Move round my wondrous existence,
The daily deep of my life ;
Prospects of things that shall be
In the country over the waves—
Memories, sorrows, and thoughts—
Noble and beautiful words,
Deeds that darkly reveal
The transparent measureless depth
Of the soul of our nature's Redeemer.
   Oh for the day that shall teach me
   To know their meaning at last,
   Beyond the lake of this life,
   Beyond the gate of the sunset
      Upon the hyaline sea!

A PRAYER.

OH, when my hour is come, if so Thou wilt,
Let the sweet blossoms of the bough of love
Hang o'er my bed.   But, howsoe'er it be,
'Thro' the night watches, till the birds awake
Their sad importunate music, till the morn
Pale on the pane, oh, let me wait for God!
Gently, my Saviour! stand beside the door ;
Gently, my Saviour! through the lattice glide ;
Dip my life's leaves, adust with thought and care,
In sacramental dews, and make them gold.
Rest over me in love, O piercèd One!
Smile on me sadly through my mist of sin,
Smile on me sweetly from Thy crown of thorns.
As the dawn looketh on the great dark hills,
As the hills dawn-touch'd on the great dark sea,
Dawn on my heart's great darkness, Prince of Peace!

WAVES, WAVES, WAVES.

WAVES, waves, waves,
Graceful arches lit with night's pale gold,
Boom like thunder thro' the mountain roll'd ;
Hiss, and make their music manifold,
Sing, and work for God along the strand.

Leaves, leaves, leaves,
Beautified by Autumn's withering breath ;
Ivory skeletons, carven fair by death,
Float and drift at a sublime command.

Thoughts, thoughts, thoughts,
Beating wavelike on the mind's strange shore,
Rustling leaf-like through it evermore—
Oh that they might follow God's good hand !

BELOW AND ABOVE.

Down below, the wild November whistling,
  Thro' the beech's dome of burning red,
And the Autumn sprinkling penitential
  Dust and ashes on the chestnut's head.

Down below, a pall of airy purple
  Darkly hanging from the mountain side,
And the sunset from his eyebrow staring
  O'er the long roll of the leaden tide.

Up above, the tree with leaf unfading
  By the everlasting river's brink,
And the sea of glass, beyond whose margin
  Never yet the sun was known to sink.

Down below, the white wings of the sea-bird,
  Dash'd across the furrows dark with mould,
Flitting like the memories of our childhood
  Through the trees now waxen pale and old.

Down below, imaginations quivering
  Through our human spirits like the wind,
Thoughts that toss like leaves about the woodland,
  Hopes like sea-birds flash'd across the mind.

Up above, the host no man can number,
  In white robes, a palm in every hand,
Each some work sublime for ever working
  In the spacious tracts of that great land.

Up above, the thoughts that know not anguish,
  Tender care, sweet love for us below,
Noble pity free from anxious terror,
  Larger love without a touch of woe.

Down below, a sad mysterious music,
  Wailing through the woods, and on the shore;
Burden'd with a grand majestic secret
  That keeps sweeping from us evermore.

Up above, a music that entwineth
  With eternal threads of golden sound
The great poem of this strange existence,
  All whose wondrous meaning has been found.

Down below, the church to whose poor window
  Glory by the autumnal trees is lent,
And a knot of worshippers in mourning,
  Missing some one at the Sacrament.

Up above, the burst of Hallelujah,
  And (without the sacramental mist
Wrapt around us like a sunlit halo)
  The great vision of the face of Christ.

Down below, cold sunlight on the tombstones
  And the green wet turf with faded flowers—
Winter roses, once like young hopes burning,
  Now beneath the ivy dripp'd with showers.

And the new-made grave within the churchyard,
  And the white cap on that young face pale,
And the watcher, ever as it dusketh,
  Rocking to and fro with that long wail.

Up above, a crown'd and happy spirit,
  Like an infant in the eternal years,
Who shall grow in love and light for ever,
  Order'd in his place among his peers.

O the sobbing of the winds of Autumn,
  And the sunset streak of stormy gold,
And the poor heart thinking in the churchyard,
  "Night is coming, and the grave is cold"!

O the pale and plash'd and sodden'd roses,
  And the desolate heart that grave above,
And the white cap shaking as it darkens
  Round that shrine of memory and love!

O the rest for ever, and the rapture,
  And the hand that wipes the tears away,
And the golden homes beyond the sunset,
  And the hope that watches o'er the clay!

All Saints' Day, 1857.

ROBERT BURNS.

SCOTLAND, meet nurse of the poetic spirit,
　　Gave to the boy his lyre;
From whose wild heart her ballad-bards inherit
　　Their pathos and their fire.

She did but touch them with her inspiration,
　　Put harps into their hand;
There was enough of love, and indignation,
　　And legend in the land.

To them the "gurly" ocean brought a wailing
　　Of girls in "kames o' goud;"
"Sir Patrick and our true loves are not sailing"
　　Home, for the sea's their shroud.

Fair Elfland's Queen, when summer twilight brought her,
　　Rode through the diamond dew;
The jingling spurs were out by Eden water,
　　Moss-troopers not a few.

The slow pathetic strain went dying, dying,
　　Griefless at last to be,
Turf-happ'd and sound asleep, with Helen lying
　　On fair Kirkconnel lea.

She lends its crimson glory to the heather,
　Mist wraps the hills afar,
Blends natural and human things together,
　Storm, sunshine, love, and war.

Mother of many songs on field and ocean,
　Lost love that weeps and yearns,
Mother of homely faith and high devotion,
　And most of Robert Burns.

All Scottish legends did his fancy fashion,
　All airs that richly flow,
Laughing with frolic, tremulous with passion,
　Broken with love-lorn woe :

Ballads whose beauties years have long been stealing
　And left few links of gold,
Under his quaint and subtle touch of healing
　Grew fairer, not less old.

Grey Cluden, and the vestals' choral cadence,
　His might awoke therewith ;
Till boatmen hung their oars to hear the maidens
　Upon the banks of Nith.

His, too, the strains of battle nobly coming
　From Bruce, or Wallace wight,
Such as the Highlander shall oft be humming
　Before some famous fight.

Nor only these—for him the hawthorn hoary
　Was with new wreaths enwrought,
The crimson-tippèd daisy wore fresh glory,
　Born of poetic thought.

From the "wee cow'ring beastie" he could borrow
  A moral strain sublime,
A noble tenderness of human sorrow,
  In wondrous wealth of rhyme.

Oh but the mountain breeze must have been pleasant,
  Upon the sunburnt brow
Of that poetic and triumphant peasant
  Driving his laurell'd plough !

Him on whom Heav'n bestow'd the heart's fine flashes,
  The lyrist's delicate art ;
While man wrote out for symbol on his ashes
  A broken lyre and heart.

Yea, and himself of wassail, praise, and passion,
  Drank deeply in his years,
And thereof for his future fame did fashion
  A veil of smiles and tears.

Smiles for the song that hath such rare beguilement,
  Laughter, and love to win ;
Tears for the dust, and ashes, and defilement,
  Tears for the shame and sin.

O the wild wit that mars the holy hymning !
  The stains upon the stole !
The spray-drops from the sea of passion dimming
  The windows of the soul !

Hush ! the man's sighs, his longings, and his laughter
  Are silent now by Doun ;
The music of the immortal song lives after,
  A many mingled tune.

And all at last, with solemn sweet surprises,
  In anthems die away,
And o'er the glee of Tam O' Shanter rises
  The " Cotter's Saturday."

And from a multitude beside the river,
  And on the mountain sod,
Sweetly goes up for ever, and for ever,
  "Come, let us worship God."

A THOUGHT FOR THE ROYAL BRIDAL.

ALL winter long
I tarried in a strange, monotonous land,
Among pine forests—an eternal throng
Of green plumes, changeless o'er the changeless sand,
Whereto the ocean singeth one sole song,
    Heard swinging heavily by sun or star,
    On its Biscayan bar.

But with the spring
I see the mountains topp'd with sunny white,
Like silver clouds beyond imagining,
Rise in the cloudless blue, and, day or night,
'Tis sweet to hear clear-water'd Adour sing,
And watch the shadows which far forests throw
    On Pyrenean snow.

All the year through
There hung a grand monotony of grief
O'er England, ever quiet, ever true.
Speeches and elegies perchance were brief,
But voices faltered, till the whole world knew
    She mourn'd her Prince—from evil tongues secure
    Because his heart was pure.

K

Worthy to bear
' Half the Crown's crushing burden in the State
Where monarchy but cometh forth more fair
From fires of revolution, where to fate
The king may yield; but still the throne is there,
        As drops that make the rainbow on the river
        Perish—the rainbow never!

        But lo! with spring
(I will not say our grief hath fled for good,
But it is time-touch'd to a gentler thing),
The Princess comes whose noble womanhood
Is better than the circlet of a king:
        Surely young grass and flowers are clothing now
        The furrows of God's plough.

        Ah! Princess, come!
Come, Princess! in the war-ship, o'er the wave;
Come, Princess! o'er the favourable foam;
With blazing streets, with banners of the brave,
With arches they will hail thee to thy home;
        With these, and the long thunders of the cheers
        Falling in rain of tears.

        In tears!—in tears!—
Remembering who, with pageantry as grand,
Pass'd through the acclaim of people and of peers,
When, with her princely spouse at her right hand,
She went in state among the endless cheers,
        And "let her people see her" as she rolled
        On, in a cloud of gold.

        Sweet lady! pass
On to St. George's Chapel. Wear as free
The royal jewels, in a starry mass

Clustered, as doth some bride of low degree
Her wreath from orchard or from meadow-grass.
    Surely when joy so trembles to a tear
    The dead are strangely near.

    From where his true
Heart-love of beauty feeds on the uncreated
And ancient Beauty that is ever new;
Where his deep thirst for purity is sated,
And his high soul hath found a work to do
    Sublimer than the work on earth he wrought,
    And full of nobler thought ;

    Surely one spirit,
Full of a tender care that is not dread,
Full of sweet love that doth no touch inherit
Of fear or woe—one of the living dead,
Stoled in the robe made white by Christ's dear merit,
    With benediction for the princely pair,
    Stands on the altar stair.

    Here, missing sore
Old England, and her streets ablaze with lights,
The illumination, when the day is o'er,
Shall be the splendours that on starry nights
From silver snows stream to heaven's silver floor ;
    And for a nation's cheers, the silent prayer
    Breath'd on the mountain air.

Bagnères de Bigorre, 1861.

A CONTRAST.*

I

OUTSIDE, over the lea,
Thunderous sky of a May-day morn,
Soft sad green of the growing corn,
The blackbird under the red-leaf'd tree,
A host of cowslips where shadows pass
From sailing clouds above the grass.
Things of the spring and summer born,
Nothing faded, nothing forlorn,
But all looks tenderly for me
Outside, over the lea.

II.

Far away a room I see.
An old man lying in mortal pain,
With thin hands clasp'd again and again.
One chant only cometh to me—
Miserere Domine !
All is vanity !
Far away a room I see.

* Written on a railway journey to attend a death-bed.

III.

Yet over sorrow and over death
Cometh at last a song that saith—
 This, this is the victory,
 Even our faith.
Love maketh all the crooked straight,
And love bringeth love to all that wait,
And laughter and light and dewy tear
 To the hard blind eyes of Fate.
All shall look tenderly yet and free
 Outside over the lea,
And deep within the heart of me.

THE ICEBOUND SHIP.

A LYRICAL FRAGMENT.

THREE things are stately found—
Yea, four, one saith, be comely in their going,
  The lion, and the he-goat, and the hound,
And, with his flying flags and bugles blowing,
  The king in harness marching, mail'd and crown'd.
    Stately is each of these;
  But statelier still the battle ship,
When o'er the white line of the heavy seas,
    Like stars o'er snow-crown'd trees,
Storm-sway'd and swung, its bright lights roll and dip.
    And statelier yet again
The spirits of our sailor Englishmen.
Well-pleased with forward ocean's manly roar,*
    They only fear the shore.

    *   *   *   *   *

    These things are stately found;
But when the lion slowly, slowly dies,
  Never waxing well of his deep wound;
When the he-goat on the golden altar lies,
  Fasten'd to it for a sacrifice;
  When the baying of the hound

* Κτύπος ἄρσην πόντου. Sophoc., Phil., 1455.

Never more beneath the hunter's glad blue skies
To the merry, merry bugle shall make full answer rise
On the field, or by the yellowing forest skirt,
Dying of a deadly hurt,
From the storm of chase apart,
With a horn-thrust in his stout old heart;
When the king, who march'd forth mail'd and crown'd,
With roses rain'd from balconies and clarion's ringing sound,
Hath red drops upon his battle shirt,
Bleeds away into his silver mail,
Sees his banners like a tatter'd sail,
And the oldest captain's cheek turns pale;
When those desperate horsemen charge, and fail,
And himself is taken by the foe and bound;—
He-goat, lion, king, and hound,
Statelier far, and nobler are ye found—
Statelier far, and nobler thus—
Beauty and glory are less glorious,
Less beautiful than sorrow, grand and true;
The steadfast will is more august than fate,
And they who greatly suffer are more great
Than they who proudly do! . . .

    *   *   *   *   *

And when the man-of-war
No longer takes the tide on her dark hull,
Nor, like a sea-bird, dippeth beautiful
Bows under to the green seas rolling far;
And heareth nevermore, the hardy tar,
The wind that singeth to the Polar star
Humming and snoring thro' rigging and spar;
But, like a grand and worn-out battle car,
The good ship rests with crystals round the keel,
And frost-flowers hanging from the wheel;

And when the man-of-war
Rests ice-bemarbled, she is statelier there,
As the crusader, carven still and fair,
With those white hands of prayer,
Is holier than the soldier fiery soul'd,
Glimmering in steel and gold—
O red-cross knight! O red-cross ship! enough ye both have
toil'd.
And the funeral bell hath toll'd,
And wave and battle both away have roll'd,
The ocean's billow and the banner's fold,
The great white horses and the rider bold.
Ah! sea and war have now no troubling breath.
Brave knight! good ship! ye surely are assoil'd
By the great pardoner—Death.

＊　　＊　　＊　　＊　　＊

Stately! but statelier yet,
What time the winter thy good ships beset
With ice-mail'd meshes of his awful net,
And wondrously the summer sun went down,
Tiara'd with the shadow and the flame—
And night with horror of great darkness came,
On her black horse, a veil upon her face,
Riding above his sunken crown.—
But day's white palfrey kept not equal pace.
Seal, and bear, and walrus brown,
Were heard no longer on the floe;
Sledge or kayak of the Esquimaux
Come there never to that place of woe;
Ptarmigan and grouse were fleck'd with snow,
All the ivory gulls flapp'd far away;
Fox and hare, turn'd white and silver-grey,
Crept in silence closer to the day.

Silence—silence—save the ice that growl'd,
Save the wind that hammer'd the stiff shroud,
Or, like lean dogs, thro' the darkness howl'd,
Hunting on some weird and wolfish cloud.
      Ah, me ! the wise men tell,
Who read the dark speech of the fossil well,
      How in some age Æonian,
      The mild moons, as 'twere queens at play,
Shook out their splendours like a silver fan,
And delicate ammonites boated in the bay,
And on the beach, through crimson-creeper'd plant
And rainbow-colour'd shell, there trode the elephant.
      At last an orange band,
     Set in a dawn of ashen grey,
To things that winter in that dreadful land
Told, like a prophet, of the sun at hand ;
And the light flicker'd like an angel's sword,
This way, and that, across the dark fiord ;
      And strangely colour'd fires
Play'd round magnificent cathedral spires,
Grandly by winter of the glacier built,
With fretted shafts by summer glory tipp'd,
And darkness was unmuffled, and was ripp'd
      Like crape from heaven's jewell'd hilt.
O those grand depths on depths that look like fate
Awfully calm and uncompassionate !
Those nights that are but clasps, or rather say
Bridges of silver flung from day to day ;
That vault which deepens up, and endeth never ;
      That sea of starlit sky,
Broad'ning and bright'ning to infinity,
Where nothing trembles, suffers, weeps for ever !
But still the ships were fast in the icefield,
And, while the midnight Arctic sun outwheel'd,

Thicker and thicker did Death's shadows fall
On the calm forehead of the Admiral.
O Admiral, thou hadst a shrine
Of silver not from any earthly mine,
Of silver ice divine—
A sacrament, but not of bread and wine.
Thou hadst the Book, the stars in whose broad skies
Are truths and silences, and mysteries,
The love which whoso loveth never dies.
Brave hearts! he cannot stay;
Only at home ye will be sure to say
How he has wrought and sought, and found—found what?
The bourne whence traveller returneth not!
Ah no! 'tis only that his spirit high
Hath gone upon a new discovery,
A marvellous passage on a sea unbounded,
Blown by God's gentle breath;
But that the white sail of his soul has rounded
The promontory—Death!

    *   *   *   *   *

How shall we bury him?
Where shall we leave the old man lying?
With music in the distance dying—dying,
Among the arches of the Abbey grand and dim;
There, if we might, we would bury him;
And comrades of the sea should bear his pall;
And the great organ should let rise and fall
The requiem of Mozart, the " Dead March " in *Saul*—
Then, silence all!
And yet far grandlier will we bury him.
Strike the ship-bell slowly—slowly—slowly!
Sailors! trail the colours half-mast high;
Leave him in the face of God most holy,
Underneath the vault of Arctic sky.

Let the long, long darkness wrap him round,
By the long sunlight be his forehead crown'd.
For cathedral panes ablaze with stories,
  For the tapers in the nave and choir,
Give him lights auroral—give him glories
  Mingled of the rose, and of the fire.
Let the wild winds like chief mourners walk,
Let the stars burn o'er his catafalque.
Hush! for the breeze, and the white fog's swathing sweep.
I cannot hear the simple service read.
Was it " earth to earth " the captain said,
Or, " we commit his body to the deep,"
    Till seas give up their dead?

   *   *   *   *   *

  Well pleased our island-mother scans,
  As mothers of heroic children use,
In things like these, her silent Inkermanns,
  Her voiceless Trafalgars, and Waterloos.
O trenches of the winter wild and black !
O Balaklavas of the rolling pack !
O combats in the sledge, or on the yards,
Magnificent as marches of the Guards !
O dreader sights to see, and sounds to list,
Than Muscovite and gun, grey through the morning mist !
Ye tell our England that of many a son
Deep agonies are suffer'd, high deeds done,
Whereof is sparing memory, or none,
That have eternity and deathless land
Before the starry threshold of our God ;
And evermore in such she learns to read
    The pledge of future deed.

   *   *   *   *   *

Hush !   Be not overbold.
Who dares to talk about success
In presence of that solemn blessedness ?
Who, but God, dares to give a martyr gold ?
        O high and stately things,
    Are ye dead—defeated still ?
Is the lion silent on the hill ?
Doth the he-goat lie before the fane,
All his glory dash'd with a red stain,
        Dropping from the heart's deep springs ?
Is the good hound mute upon the track ?
Is the mail'd king borne thro' tears that fall like rain,
        Drums and banners muffled up in black ?
Is the war-ship frozen up for ever ?
Shall the sailor see home's white cliffs never ?
Hush ! Oh, leave him in the darkness of the land,
        Cover'd with the shadow of Christ's hand ;
        Leave him in the midnight Arctic sun,
        God's great light o'er duty nobly done,
        God's great whiteness for the pardon won ;
Leave him waiting for the setting of the Throne,
Leave him waiting for the trumpet to be blown,
        In God's bosom, in a land unknown.
    Leave him (he needeth no lament)
        With suns, and nights, and snow ;
Life's tragedy is more magnificent,
Ending with that sublime and silent woe.
        'Tis well it should be so.

1858.

PICTURA POESIS.

GENOA, 1872.

Two sunny winter days I sped along
   The Riviera's winding mountain way;
Scarcely I caught the blue sea's faint far song,
   By terraced hill and olive-shaded bay.

Far off the Alpine snow's eternal line
   Stretch'd over hills with wondrous curves cut well,
Against the irridescent dome divine,
   The cupola of light ineffable.

They say thought loses 'neath the Italian heaven
   The mortal languor of its modern scorn;
That England's passionless pilgrims may be given
   An ampler soul beneath an ampler morn.

Would it were thus!   In sooth it may be so,
   Yet well I ween, my littleness I bore
In sight of the imperishable snow,
   In presence of the glory of that shore,

—Selfish before that purity without end,
   Faith's eye ungifted with a sight more keen,
What time the outward eye had fullest kenn'd
   Those long deep distances of lustrous sheen.

False where our God so many a secret writes
　　In lovely syllables for souls elect,
Aye, where the very winter half his nights
　　In gardens sleeps of roses not undeck'd.

If he have wrinkles, they are greenly hid ;
　　If murmurings, they are tuned to silver seas ;
And any dimness from his brow is chid
　　By the gold lamps of all the orange trees.

And so we came to that world-famous sweep
　　Where, on her amphitheatre of hill,
Old Genoa looks superbly on the deep,
　　As if she held her own Columbus still ;

As if toward Africa, at close of day,
　　Her galleys headed under press of sail,
And brave old Admiral Doria, grim and grey,
　　Watch'd from the terraces their golden trail,

And to the gentle girl who paced beside
　　Told tales of sinking ships and war clouds dun,
Until he heard again the hurrying tide
　　And the long growling of the battle gun.

Yet still, through all the witchery of the clime,
　　My heart felt burden'd with its former pain ;
I ask'd for something beyond reach of time,
　　To make me for a little young again.

Nor ask'd in vain,—for wandering here and there,
　　To see the pictures with an idle heart,
Above the red Palazzo's marble stair
　　I own'd the magic of old Vandyck's art.

Be still, and let me gaze—a noble child
  Upon the Master's canvas here I see :
Surely two hundred summer suns have smiled
  Italian light, young Brignola, on thee.

The light that makes such violets divine,
  And hangs such roses on the haunted soil,
And spheres such flashes in the flask of wine,
  And fills the olive with such golden oil.

The light, too, that makes hearts with living chords
  Too fine for happiness—that never fails
To ripen lives too richly—whence the words
  Of all those strange pathetic passion tales.

But thou, immortal child ! with those dark eyes,
  And that proud brow—I will not call it white,—
A something rather like the snow that lies
  Between dark clouds and the unclouded light.

I know not, will not ask what was thy fate—
  Whether thou laughedst in this very spot,
Then wentest forth in beauty with thy mate,
  A fair adventure and a gentle lot.

Whether with intermingling gleam and gloom
  Thy shadows and thy sunshine did rain down,
Like that sweet lady in the other room,
  Thy sister with the gold on her green gown.

Whether thou livedst till the winter came,
  And the calm with it that its spring denies,
Retaining only of thy present frame
  The unextinguish'd light of those full eyes.

Whether thou lovedst, and the winds of heaven
  Blew favourably,—and, thy moon-touch'd sail
Glimm'ring into the dark, to thee was given
  The voyage of a little fairy tale.

Whether thou lovedst—after that forlorn
  Tasting the bitter out of human sweet,
Thy forehead pierced with some acanthus thorn,
  The cruel thistles stabbing all thy feet,

Till, as befalls in this strange land of thine,
  Where prayer and passion, earth and heav'n so mix,
A mournful thing thou fledd'st to love divine,
  And found'st a bridegroom in the crucifix.

But as it is, thou standest here for aye,
  Type of the gracious childhood of the south,
Thy dark hair never fleck'd with threads of grey,
  No channell'd lines under thy perfect mouth.

Thou hast no grief, no selfishness at all.
  Possessing all of beauty but its scorn,
Thou floatest smilingly outside the fall,
  Unsuffering, unsinning, unforlorn.

I cannot question thee—if thou couldst speak
  Thy soft Italian would but touch mine ears
As if a sweet wind beat upon my cheek
  Through the dim light a rain of flowers and tears.

Enough that, wrought by Vandyck's master hand,
  I see thy beauty by an inward light,
And in a better language understand
  Thy childhood's inextinguishable light.

ADRIFT ON THE ARCTIC SEA.

I SEE a ship adrift upon the tide,
   Methinks she maketh past King William's Land ;
The stars are glimmering through her rifted side,
   Her mast is like a giant's broken wand.

What, is there no one standing at the wheel ?
   An awful ship indeed without a stir ;
Yet through the icebergs steers the rolling keel,
   Like death's pale horses panting after her.

Well done, O silent ship ! the bar is past,
   The icy battlement left upon the lee ;
Why doth no gallant sailor climb the mast
   To view the glory of that iceless sea ?

O silent ship and crew ! the starriest crown
   Of all earth's mariners your deed hath won ;
But lo ! the ship first reels, and then goes down,
   And with her all her crew—a skeleton.

So when some thinker wins the prize of thought,
   And his keel cuts the just-discover'd wave,
Down with him goes the work that he has wrought—
   He finds at once a passage and a grave.

L

PAINTING FOR TIME.

One sunny eventide,
At a great painter's side,
A maiden paced glad eyed.
Enchanted did she see
That glorious gallery.
Beauty and strength were there,
The heroic and the fair,
Faces superbly wrought
By the creative thought.
Happy she walk'd, and proud,
Yet something like a cloud
Just touch'd the maiden's brow.
Quoth he, " What thinkest thou ? "
" Master," she said, " this place
Is haunted with all grace.
There, where shafts falling late
Those forms irradiate,
Lo ! as I gaze, they seem
To pass into a dream.
A dream—but, as men say,
Ere sea-frets gather grey,
While still is light to scan,
That stream Northumbrian,*

* The Coquet at Warkworth, famous for the peculiar definiteness of
the shadows which it reflects.

The shadow of the spire,
And the autumn trees on fire
Look as real as the things
 To our imaginings.
So gazing here I think,
As by that river's brink
Shadow and substance stand
Inverted by thy hand—
The shadows I and you,
They only fix'd and true,
They those alone who live,
And we insubstantive,
Yet on their features all
Whose semblance fills the hall
Why hath thy hand let fall
That wanness as of snow?
Master, I long to know."

 " Heed not what now appears
In the abyss of years;
In the unapparent morn
Of centuries unborn,
Something more fair and fine
Than thou canst now divine;
Some magic colour thrown
On the white monotone,
Some unimagined dye
Under the distant sky
Of the futurity,
Shall yet unlighted eyes
Transcendently surprise.
Say not—*this colouring pale
Is but of small avail.
The hues thou dost create
Are too immaculate.*

Flood them with warmer flood,
Paint with more passionate blood,
As with red grape's rich juice
The whiteness interfuse.
Men generations hence
Shall thank my abstinence
Prophetic and sublime."
He cried, " I paint for time,
And these shall live in light,
Ideal and infinite
Of dawns when I lie dead.
I paint for time," he said.

Laughter, or love, or tears,
Who would bequeath his peers,
Far through the distant years ;
Who would a work descry
Man's heart will not let die,
While lives mortality ;
He with an aim sublime
Must also paint for time,
And proudly wise let fall
Applauses temporal.

NARROW GOODNESS.

As a child, in a quiet place
    Which earth's wild whirl hath hardly stirr'd,
    Grows shy as some fair forest bird,
And feareth every stranger's face,

And wots not what a world there is
    Of love beyond his little isle,
    Half jealous of his father's smile,
Half jealous of his mother's kiss;

But when he leaves that strip of strand,
    Life's larger continent to explore,
    He findeth friends on the far shore,
And graspeth many a brother's hand:

So may I deem it fares with thee—
    So may I think that thou hast found,
    O man of God! who standest crown'd
With glory on the crystal sea!

Where all the harps are heavenly sweet,
    Where all the palms are passing green;
    Where on all faces falls the sheen
Of the temple in the golden street;

Are hands thou never thought'st would fold
  The heavenly harp, the fadeless palm,
  And faces most divinely calm
Thou never thoughtest to behold.

Forgive, if in thy textual art
  I see thee what thou art not now,
  With something of a narrow brow
And something of a narrow heart;

If any buds that thou hast strewn
  To me look dry for want of showers,
  And scentless as Platonic flowers,
Pale white beneath the pale white moon.*

For still, I think, in world's above
  The narrow brow grows bright and broad
  With the great purposes of God,
And the heart widens with His love.

And the poor thoughts on earth so pale,
  Turn to the sun his warmth to win,
  And drink the silent sunbeams in,
And hue and fragrance never fail.

, Sure at thy creed, confess'd erewhile,
  Now with large heart and lovelit eye
  Thou sighest—if the blessèd sigh;
Thou smilest—if the blessèd smile.

Thou smilest at the glory given
  To those innumerable kings,
  And putt'st away thy childish things,
Taught by the manly love of Heaven;

* Platonici flores quosdam etiam lunæ dicunt esse familiares, qui
sanè huic sideri canant hymnos. (Scaliger, " De Subtil," Ex. 170.)

For whilst that thou wert here below,
  From that thick-thorn'd belief of thine
  Thy spirit push'd some flowers divine,
Like furze that flowers in frost and snow.

And as, when finest fancies troop
  Across the painter's haunted soul,
  He draws the outline first in coal
Before he lets the pencil droop

With colour like the sky above:
  So dark the sketch thy heart had drawn—
  But now it wears the rose-red dawn,
Or floats in golden mists of love.

So let me think for evermore,
  Yea, let me say beside the sea—
  "God's love is singing loud to me,
And chanting grandly on the shore."

And say, when all the stars are high—
  "It is our Father's ancient book.
  How many myriad myriads look
On His love-letters of the sky!"

And say, where anguish never sleeps,
  Staring upon the city wall,
  Where, shaking in her gaudy shawl,
On the door-step the harlot weeps,—

"Father! I know Thee good as just!
  O Dove Divine, I hear Thy wings
  Come rustling round these faded things,
And dropping dew upon their dust!

" I hear Thee whispering unto sin,
   I see Thee in the flowerlike thought
   That groweth in such hearts unsought,
For which they neither toil nor spin.

" I see, too, where, with lifted hands,
   Amidst all shapes of human woe,
   A heavenly shadow on life's snow,
The Christus Consolator stands."

So let me say, and let me feel
   That through all sin our Father's eye
   Looks love on all beneath the sky,
That He is willing all should kneel.

And let me hope some trembling souls
   May enter Heaven from this cold world,
   Like poor birds by the snow-wind hurl'd
In where the great church organ rolls :

Although they know not where they fly,
   Although they open their dim eyes,
   All panting with the great surprise,
The grand and awful harmony.

THE PREACHER'S MEDITATION.

1.

Lord of all these thousand spirits,
  spirits differing more than faces do;
Knowing all these thousand spirits,
  with their thousand histories, through and through;
Knowing all these thousand histories
  as their own hearts know not—never knew;—

2.

Save me from the mean ambition
  vulgar praise of eloquence to win—
From falsetto and self-conscious
  pathos—from declamatory din—
From the tricky pulpit business,
  and the silky talking that is sin.

3.

Grant me honestly and strongly,
  as the strong and honest only can,
To uprear my temple.   Ever
  when a great cathedral stands for man,
Still, severe, serene, and simple,
  depth of thought and science drew the plan.

4.

Save me from false intermixture,
　faithless patronizing of Thy grace.
From the too resplendent colours
　that the tender tints of truth efface,
From the insolent scorn unholy
　of Thy glorious holy commonplace.

5.

Never yet hath earthly chemist
　secret of creating gem-stars found ;
Still the difficult tint mysterious
　lies uncaught—for God takes half the round
Of the ages for creating
　the small deathless light call'd diamond.

6.

Never yet hath earthborn message,
　chemistry, or stroke of chisel faint,
Lit and glorified our nature,
　made the gem without a flaw or taint :
All God's working, and His only,
　makes that diamond divine—a saint.

7.

Never bright point but the gospel's
　won all colours hidden in heart deeps,
Show'd in perfected reflection
　all that nobly flashes, sweetly weeps.
—So they say the sea-tinct sapphire
　somewhere in the blood-blush'd ruby sleeps.

8.

Wherefore not at all I ask Thee
    for the sharp-cut facets of bright wit—
Not for arrows of the archer
    cunning that the inner circle hit—
Not for colour'd fountains rising
    by fantastic lamps and glasses lit.

9.

If Thy Spirit's sword-hilt glitter
    sometimes, as its blade divine I wheel,
Golden thought or gemlike fancy
    is not God's own sharpness.   Soldier leal
Thinks not of the gold and jewell'd
    hilt, but of the keenness of the steel.

10.

Grant me, Lord, in all my studies,
    through all volumes roaming where I list,
Whatsoever spacious distance
    rise in ample grandeur through thought's mist,
Whatsoever land I find me,
    that of right divine to claim for Christ.

11.

Do men dare to call Thy Scripture—
    mystic forest, unillumined nook?
If it be so, O my spirit!
    then let Christ arise on thee, and look!
With the long lane of His sunlight
    shall be cut the forest of His Book.

12.

And at times give me the trembling
  inevitable words that none forget.
Give the living golden moment
  when a thousand eyes are lit and wet,
And some pathos makes the silence
  palpitate, and grow more silent yet.

13.

And a thousand hearts together
  are as one love-fused and reconciled.
And a thousand passionate natures
  harden'd by the world and sin-defiled,
Look upon me for a moment
  with the soft eyes of a little child.

14.

Give me words like the unveiling
  lightning that the sky a moment rips—
Words that show the world eternal
  over where this world's horizon dips—
Words of more than magic music,
  with the name of Jesus on the lips.

15.

Give me words of Thine to utter
  that shall open the lock'd heart like keys,—
Words that, like Thine own sweet teaching,
  shall be medicinal for disease,—
Words like a revolving lanthorn
  for the ships in darkness—give me these.

16.

In the Sunday summer evening
  two lights are there, in the church, unlike.
One the cool sweet dying sunshine ;
  one the gas-jets' fierce light-beaded spike.
With the first my speech be gifted—
  light to touch and tremble, not to strike.

17.

So for all these thousand spirits,
  differing more than any faces do,
Christ through me may have some message
  that shall be at once both old and new,
And my sinful human brethren
  through my sinful lips learn something true.

IMPERFECT REPENTANCE.

AT such a time—full well I know within
    Myself—I wrought a sin.
Light in the eye it had, and little sips
    Of honey on the lips.
No sooner done but the light died, and all
    The honey became gall.
Then was my soul stone-silent for a space,
    And whiteness wann'd my face.

After a little then again I heard
    The music of the word,
And took the absolution sweet and grand
    Into my own faith's hand,
And breathed the ozone in the healing breeze
    Of sacramental seas.
Out rang my song : " My sore distress doth cease,
    Pardon I find and peace ;
The very plenitude of Love divine
    Unboundedly is mine."

But lo ! the step of Time steals slowly on,
    And, ever and anon,
The spectre of the sin which I thought lost
    Rises, no hated ghost.

Rather, " How beautiful," my spirit cries,
   " O love ! are those grey eyes.
What filmy robes float for me, what rich tunes,
   Dim fields and white half-moons.
And, while some silver flax-rock in the brown
   Rack is turn'd upside down,
The fine disorder'd threads and cloud-fluff thin
   Are like thy hair, sweet sin !
And, as we pass, the faint scent rises yet
   Of stock and mignonette,
Through the garden looking on the starlit sea—
   And my sin kisseth me.
And twice as fair she is as ever of old,
   Because not half so bold,—
The grossness of the sense and of the eye
   Refined to memory ;
The ethereal delicacy of the past
   Over fact's coarse world cast ;
The flexile bough of fancy quivering on
   After the bird is gone."

Whereon I thought—" Alas ! the heavy fall.
   I am not changed at all.
Look how some fitful hour when smoky grey
   Mountain-mists roll away,
The sunshine's magic and creative sports
   Transform white seams of quartz,
Whereof each one that glistens, being wetted,
   Seemeth with diamonds fretted,
But, being dried and unlit, it is found
   Mere stone, not diamond,—
So seem'd I like a saint upon God's hill
   That am a sinner still.

Methought that I, out of the strong black jaw
    And iron grasp of law,
Had pass'd over the poor earthly line
    Into the land divine,
Where all things are made new, and grace redresses
    Us with her tendernesses.
Ah ! I who loved the living love its ghost,
    And, loving, I am lost.

What shall I say ?--that thoughts like these returning
    Are scarcely worth the mourning,—
Nay, that they have a beauty in their place,
    Disgracing not my grace,
Like green corn-ears ungilded of the suns
    Bettering the golden ones ?
Not this shall be my argument—but this :
    " See lest thy crown thou miss ;
And, that thou hear not one day bitter sentence,
    Repent of thy repentance."

II.

CHARACTERS, INSCRIPTIONS,

ETC.

R. C. TRENCH, ARCHBISHOP OF DUBLIN.

RESIGNED NOVEMBER 28, 1884.

"Laureatus spiritu scriptis coronatur suis."

THOU whom we miss and mourn,
Though not yet graveward borne,
Who by this act of faith
Hast antedated death,—
Thee our love speaks about,
As if thy presence out
Had stately to the vast
Darkness and silence pass'd;
As if all light that lies
Deep in those thoughtful eyes,
Splendour and shadowy grace
Of that pathetic face,
All the strange music known
Unto thy voice alone,
Of prayer and sorrow born,
Mix'd with majestic scorn
Of baseness and of ill,—
As if all these were still;

As if the light and sound
Were changed for the profound
Quiet and darken'd spot
Where all things are forgot.
Thou, in all working such
As thy true hand did touch,
Thou, with an aim sublime,
Master, didst write for time.
Thou scornedst to imprint
One evanescent tint
Upon the measured page
Thou mad'st so grave and sage.
Wherefore the years shall look
With thanks upon thy book.

Thou, when an angry spell
On clamorous hundreds fell;
Or sometimes when men press'd
Thorns to that patient breast,
Or their suspicion laid
Upon that stately head,
Slowly didst turn away
Heart-wounded from the fray,
And unto God alone
Madest majestic moan.

God! by whose will created
The time and man are mated,
Give us such chiefs again,
Give us such kings of men
Who shout no narrow creed,
And do no little deed,
But to their work impart
A grace-touch'd human heart.

DEATH OF ARCHBISHOP WHATELY.

RICHARD WHATELY, D.D., BORN 1787, DIED 1863.

FAST falls the October rain, and dull and leaden
   Stretch the low skies, without one line of blue ;
And up the desolate streets, with sobs that deaden
   The rolling wheels, the winds come rolling too.

Faster than rain fall teardrops, bells are tolling ;
   The dark sky suits the melancholy heart ;
From the church organs awfully is rolling
   Down the draped fanes, the requiem of Mozart.

O tears beyond control of half a nation,
   O sorrowful music, what have ye to say ?
Why take men up so deep a lamentation ?
   What prince or great man hath there fall'n to-day ?

Only an old Archbishop, growing whiter
   Year after year, his stature proud and tall,
Palsied and bow'd, as by his heavy mitre ;
   Only an old Archbishop—that is all !

Only the hands that held with feeble shiver
   The marvellous pen—by others outstretch'd o'er
The children's heads—are folded now for ever
   In an eternal quiet—nothing more !

No martyr he, o'er fire and sword victorious ;
  No saint in silent rapture kneeling on ;
No mighty orator with voice so glorious
  That thousands sigh when that sweet voice is gone.

Yet in Heaven's great cathedral, peradventure,
  There are crowns rich above the rest, with green
Places of joy peculiar where they enter
  Whose fires and swords no eye hath ever seen.

They who have known the truth, the truth have spoken
  With few to understand and few to praise,
Casting their bread on waters, half heart-broken,
  For men to find it after many days.

And better far than eloquence—that golden
  And spangled juggler dear to thoughtless youth—
The luminous style through which there is beholden
  The honest beauty of the face of Truth.

And better than his loftiness of station,
  His power of logic, or his pen of gold,
The half unwilling homage of a nation
  Of fierce extremes to one who seem'd so cold ;

The purity by private ends unblotted,
  The love that slowly came with time and tears,
The honourable age, the life unspotted,
  That is not measured merely by its years.

And better far than flowers that blow and perish
  Some sunny week the roots deep laid in mould
Of quickening thoughts, which long blue summers cherish,
  Long after he who planted them is cold.

Yea, there be saints who are not like the painted
    And haloed figures fix'd upon the pane,
Not outwardly, and visibly ensainted,
    But hiding deep the light which they contain.

The rugged gentleness, the wit whose glory
    Flash'd like a sword because its edge was keen,
The fine antithesis, the flowing story,
    Beneath such things the sainthood is not seen,

Till in the hours when the wan hand is lifted
    To take the bread and wine, through all the mist
Of mortal weariness our eyes are gifted
    To see a quiet radiance caught from Christ;

Till from the pillow of the thinker, lying
    In weakness, comes the teaching then best taught;
That the true crown for any soul in dying
    Is Christ not genius, and is faith not thought.

O wondrous lights of death, the great unveiler,
    Lights that come out above the shadowy place,
Just as the night, that makes our small world paler,
    Shows us the star-sown amplitudes of space!

Rest then, O martyr, pass'd from anguish mortal;
    Rest then, O saint, sublimely free from doubt;
Rest then, O patient thinker, o'er the portal,
    Where there is peace for brave hearts wearied out.

O long unrecognized, thy love too loving,
    Too wise thy wisdom, and thy truth too free!
As on the searchers after truth are moving,
    They may look backward with deep thanks to thee.

DEATH OF ARCHBISHOP WHATELY.

By his dear Master's holiness made holy
    All lights of hope upon that forehead broad,
Ye mourning thousands quit the Minster slowly,
    And leave the great Archbishop with his God.

DEATH OF LORD J. G. BERESFORD, PRIMATE OF ALL IRELAND.

To his rest among the saints of old
That our stately Primate must be laid,
  In an ever hallow'd mould,
That the good Archbishop sleepeth well,
Tongue and pen unto the people tell ;
Drape the great cathedral where he pray'd,
  Let the bell be toll'd.

Not for marvellous speech or musings grand,
Not for martyr's pains !   Those noble eyes
  Open'd on a golden land ;
With him beauty, honour, wealth, and power
Grew like hue and fragrance with the flower ;
Stormless, all in sunshine did he rise
  And in sunshine stand.

Taylor, round the altar twining roses,
Colour'd by the summer of his touch ;
  Ken, his music who discloses,
Half by angels, half by thrushes taught ;
Butler's regal majesty of thought,—
Ireland's princely Primate had not such :
  Weep where he reposes.

Ay, whilst now the white sail of his soul
Watch we glimmering round death's misty cape,
    Slowly let the organ roll !
From our clouded hearts let raindrops fall
To the soft breath of the ritual ;
Solemnly the old cathedral drape,
    Let the church bells toll !

Strong is eloquence, and lore is deep—
But for kingly quiet so sustain'd
    That it seem'd a saintly sleep,
For the lore that was so simply wise,
For the lordly presence and calm eyes,
For the love and purity unfeign'd,
    Let the people weep.

Not by fourteen thousand bits of gold
Measured, but by books at Resurrection
    Of the perfect just unroll'd,
Ah ! it must have been a weary weight,
Fifty years of such a high estate—
Well ! he need not fear the recollection,—
    Let the bell be toll'd.

Ah ! the great bell tolleth—there blow never
Twice the self-same flowers, but other ones ;
    Flows not twice the self-same river.
All that majesty of prayers and alms,
All that sweetness as of chanted psalms
Round the brow half princely, half St. John's,
    It is gone for ever.

Ah ! the great bell tolls, but through the cloud,
If we see aright, and through the mist,

Larger eyed and broader brow'd,
With his stainless lawn divinely brighter,
With a crown and not a heavy mitre,
In the full cathedral fane of Christ
Is the Archbishop bow'd.

Leave him with the Bishop of our souls,
Leave the princely old man with the bless'd ;
Need is none of Fame's false scrolls :
Calm is on his brow from God's own climate,
Softly draw the curtain round our Primate,
Let the angels sing him to his rest,—
Ah ! the great bell tolls !

July 26, 1862.

DEATH OF S. WILBERFORCE,
BISHOP OF WINCHESTER.

How thin the veil between our eyes,
   And angel wings in motion !
How narrow the long ledge that lies
   'Twixt us and death's dim ocean !

They rode by sunlit copse and glen
   And 'neath the woodland's shadow
They spurn'd, with hoofs that rang again,
   The cruel sloping meadow.

A plunge—a fall—and lo ! the rock.
   The veil was rent asunder.
How swift the change, how sharp the shock,
   How bright the waking yonder !

Old England heard it with a start ;
   She mourns with voice uplifted :
Mother of many a noble heart,
   But ah ! what son so gifted ?

From his own Oxford's storied hall,
   Her stream by light oars ruffled,
To where, beside the plane-trees tall,
   His Winton's bells are muffled,

The whole land wears the garb of grief
  For that great wealth departed—
Her peerless prelate, statesman, chief,
  Large soul'd and gentle hearted;

The man so eloquent of word,
  Who sway'd all spirits near him,
Who did but touch the silver chord,
  And men perforce must hear him;

Who won rude natures at his will,
  And charm'd them with the glamour
Of his sweet tongue, and kept them still
  Forgetful of their clamour;

Who from no task for Christ soe'er,
  True soldier, sought indulgence,—
To him it wore so grand an air,
  ·Was lit with such effulgence;

Who sweetly smiled, and deftly plann'd,
  And his true work to fashion,
Like hammers in a skilful hand,
  Took every party's passion;

Whom men call'd subtle overmuch
  Because all threads of beauty
He interwork'd with magic touch
  Into the web of Duty,

And from their hundred varying dyes
  Wove well a wondrous colour,
That might have pleased malignant eyes
  More, if it had been duller;

He for whom many hearts are sore,
  Lost to so many places—
The great cathedral's crowded floor
  A hush of upturn'd faces,—

The village church, where children knelt
  Beneath his hands o'ershading,
And rugged men sweet comfort felt
  Or tender true upbraiding,—

The Senate, barren evermore
  Of the rich voice that stirr'd it,—
The platform, where the charm is o'er
  That spell-bound all who heard it.

How many a noble deed he plann'd !
  How many a soul he guided,
With sympathy of heart and hand,
  And feelings many-sided !

And when the social lists were lit,
  And worthy foemen tilted,
How flash'd the poniard of his wit,
  Keen-bladed, diamond-hilted.

Sleep calm in earth, a Bishop robed,
  Waiting God's golden morrow.
O memory, leave the wound unprobed,
  Nor bring too sharp a sorrow !

Let love draw near, and hope and faith,
  Where the good saint lies sleeping ;
His white face beautiful in death,
  His soul in Christ's own keeping.

WILLIAM DERRY,
C. F. ALEXANDER.

ON READING SOME LINES BY WILLIAM ARCHER BUTLER.

As when at night we tread the lonely deck,
   In the first hour of moonlight on the wave,
Far, far away, the watcher marks some streak
   Which dying day hath pencill'd o'er his grave :

So more than living lights, beyond all fair,
   In living genius, is departed worth—
Man's spirit makes love-tokens of whate'er
   Hath come from genius now no more on earth.

As in a gold-clasp'd volume closely hid,
   The pale, pale leaves of some remember'd rose,
Dating the heart's deep chronicles unbid,
   Suggest more thought than all which greenly grows ;

As in the winter, from some marble jar,
   Whose sides are honey'd with a rosy breath,
You catch faint footfalls of the spring afar,
   And find a memory in the scent of death :

So these, the characters of Butler's pen,
   Are more to us than all that, day by day,
Are traced by mightiest hands of living men,—
   T'is death that makes them more esteem'd than they.

'Tis not because the affluent fancy flung
　　Such pearls of price ungrudging at thy feet,
'Tis not because that blessèd poet sung
　　His Heavenly Master's truth in words so sweet :

No ; 'tis because the heavy churchyard mould
　　Lies on the dear one in that lonely dell—
Lies on the hand that held the pen of gold,
　　The brain that thought so wisely, and so well.

Nay, say not so ;—write epitaphs like these
　　For sons of song who fling light words abroad,
Whose art is canker'd with a sore disease,
　　Who feed a flame that tends not up to God.

But *he*, the empurpled cross with healing shadow
　　Was the great measure of the much he knew ;
'Twas this he saw on mountain, and on meadow,
　　The only beautiful, the sternly true.

Not vague to him the great Laudate still
　　Stirring the strong ones of the waterflood,
And the deep heart of many an ancient hill,
　　And light-hung chords of every vocal wood ;—

Not dark the language written on the wide
　　Marmoreal ocean—written on the sky,
On the scarr'd volume of the mountain side,
　　On many-pagèd flowers that lowly lie ;—

Nor dark, nor vague ; not Nature, but her God ;
　　Nor only Nature's God, but Three in One,
Father, Redeemer, Comforter—bestow'd
　　On hearts made temples by the Incarnate Son.

All sweetest strains rang hollow to his ear,
   Wanting this key-note ; earthy, of the earth,
Seeming like beauty to the eye of fear,
   Like the wild anguish of a harlot's mirth.

True Poet, true Philosopher—to whom
   Beauty was one with truth, and truth with beauty ;
True Priest, no flowers so sweet upon thy tomb
   As those pure blossoms won from rugged duty.

He might have sung as precious songs as e'er
   Made our tongue golden since its earliest burst,
But those poetic wreaths him seem'd less fair
   Than moral truth o'er science wide dispersed.

He might have read man's nature deeper far
   Than any since his broad-brow'd namesake died,
But like those Eastern Sages, so the star
   He follow'd—till he found the cradle side.

And now, ye mountains and ye voiceful streams !
   For your interpreter ye need not weep ;
On the eternal hills fall brighter gleams,
   Through Eden more delightful rivers sweep.

Friends, kinsmen, fellow-churchmen, fellow-men,
   Yes, ye may weep, but be it not for him.
Life might have brought him larger lore—what then ?
   It would have kept him from the seraphim.

Dear hand, dear lines, in them still undeparted
   Tokens I see of one before the Throne,—
Butler the child-like, and the tender-hearted,
   Taken so young by Him who takes His own.

1848.

DEATH OF THE EARL OF DERBY.

"Ille ego qui quondam."

As looks a hero after fields of battle
  On those whose skill hath been the charge to shun,
On craven cohorts with unbloody armour,
  Chattering of the achievements they have done—
    A tragic look and solemn,
  Sorrow, contempt, and pity all in one :

So when those fatal nights of great debating
  And pettiest sequel paled to their last dawn,
So look'd our Derby ere he left for ever
  The red-bench'd chamber with its rows long drawn—
    Look'd on his broken party,
  Look'd ominous on the triple lines of lawn,

And then pass'd out ; but ere he left he turn'd him
  And on his gather'd Peers he gazed again—
So in the olden days some strong pathetic
  Face of a wounded prophet gazed, and then
    Sank in God's darkness grandly
  From out the infinite littleness of men,—

Pass'd from the petty policies around him
  To ampler spheres, where all is large and deep,—
Pass'd to the summer morning in its calmness,
  Colouring the space divine and skiey sweep
      O'er Westminster and London
  That starts and talks and tosses in its sleep ;—

Pass'd onward for a little, peradventure,
  To realms enchanted, loved in days gone by,
To hear the music intricate yet familiar
  That Horace meditates, or with kindling eye
      To listen to the ancient
  Majestic roll of Homer's poetry ;

Pass'd for a while to think of manly triumphs
  Won in the full assembly of the State,
Long since, when principles were powers in England,
  When parties and their orators were great,
      The golden days when Stanley
  Was still the star and marvel of debate ;

When, not with swollen limb and pallid forehead
  And faltering memory, but with faultless word
And rolling fire of eloquence and sarcasm
  He spoke the speeches that a nation heard,
      And all the stormy pulses
  Of the Commons House of Parliament were stirr'd ;—

Pass'd to the things of more abiding import,
  The silent agonies of frame and brain,
That sometimes bring the sick man from Christ's Presence
  The light that makes so many mysteries plain,
      The solemn wine of gladness
  That cometh with the sacrament of pain ;—

Pass'd to the chamber in his lordly mansion,
   Where still his mother Church with music mild
From her old book of promise and of pardon
   The weary hours of lassitude beguiled,
      And, like a soldier's mother,
   Breath'd of her sweetest to her bravest child.

Now that last look we saw upon his features
   Is surely changed into a tender bliss.
No more of scorn, or pain, or pity—something
   Gentler than arrow-touch of Artemis,*
      Repose and adoration,
   And whatsoever else immortal is.

Ah ! ye do well to bear him out from Knowsley,
   Quietly, as he charged you, to the aisle.
No harm that muffled bells be heard from steeples,
   Or that flags half-mast high be hung awhile;
      But let not any herald
   Break the wand o'er him, and proclaim his style.

Only what time the vault is dimly lighted
   Among the proud old Earls the bier be set;
And of retainer rough, and sturdy tenant,
   And noble kindred, every cheek be wet;
      And on the blazon'd coffin
   Be duly seen the cap and coronet.

Sufficient is all England's proclamation
   Of him whose chaplet many a leaf entwines—
The noblest giver of the noblest largesse;
   Whose name for ever on her record shines;
      Who, for a while turned poet,
   Pour'd his large rhetoric into Homer's lines.

* Il., xxiv. 759.

Sufficient for his witness to his country
The work that only patriot spirits can
Work in the plenitude of truth and genius,
The loftiest life-work of directest plan—
Rest, Edward, Earl of Derby,
A very perfect knight and gentleman.

THE DERRY STATUE TO THE MEMORY OF SIR R. A. FERGUSON, M.P.

Ah, raise it up—
Raise up the statue in the storied town ;
Make it a sign of sorrow and renown,
Like flags that tell us where a ship went down.

Ah, raise it up—
Raise up the statue in the quiet square ;
Crowning the street that rises, like a stair,
Up from the river in the gloom or glare.

And let it front
At eve or dawn, or with a nameless charm
Of mystic darkness on its folded arm,
The Foyle that brims and brightens by the Farm.

Why raise it up?
Where are the great lines there that we may seek,
As of the statesman with pale brow and cheek,
As of the senator in act to speak ?

Not such are here,
If life-drawn truth have moulded it ; not such,
If inspiration, by some happy touch,
Have stamp'd in bronze the presence loved so much.

> Yet raise it up.
> Methinks the shaggy brow speaks honest scorn,
> And sharp and kindly as a frosty morn
> Is the man's wholesome influence reborn.
>
> Ah, raise it up—
> Show us the rugged gentleness, the true eyes
> Of him who never wrought for place or prize,
> Who lack'd the golden eloquence—that lies !
>
> Ah, raise it up—
> And let it tell, as far as sculpture can,
> For those who have congenial hearts to scan,
> The noble quietness of an honest man.
>
> Yet scarcely tell
> The lines that gather on that kindly brow,
> The cares that wither and the pains that bow—
> He has forgotten them, and we will now.
>
> And often here,
> Come from the heather'd hill, where ever higher,
> Summer by summer, creeps the yellow fire
> Of the ripe corn right up the mountain's spire—
>
> And often here,
> When in the busy square the parted meet,
> Peasant and stately gentleman shall greet
> A face they know, a presence sadly sweet.
>
> Ah me ! ah me !
> The souls in white, who with a single aim
> Have wrought or thought for us, they may not claim
> Or care to hear the echoes of their name.

They may not heed
If men remember them or not below—
Earth's bells are muffled for them as with snow,
Perchance unheard o'er the dark river's flow.

Yet raise it up—
Raise up the statue, in this land and time,
When to tell truth heads all the lists of crime,
And lives are low, and only words sublime.

EPITAPH ON AGNES JONES.

BURIED IN FAHAN CHURCHYARD.

ALONE with Christ in this sequester'd place,
Thy sweet soul learn'd its quietude of grace.
On sufferers waiting in this vale of ours,
Thy gifted touch was train'd to higher powers ;
Therefore, when death, O Agnes ! came to thee—
Not on the cool breath of our lakelike sea,
But in the workhouse hospital's hot ward,
A gentle helper with the gentle Lord,—
Proudly as men heroic ashes claim,
We ask'd to have thy fever-stricken frame,
And lay it in our grass beside our foam,
Till Christ the Healer call His healers home.

EPITAPH ON S. M.

For a Ward of a Hospital.

Thy body rests beneath the Italian sod,
Thy soul's inheritance is the light of God ;
Yet here our hopes and memories of thee
Who sleepest well beside the far blue sea
We twine, all fair and sunny as they are,
With other sights and scenes that differ far,—
With sickness, mortal agony, and tears ;
Yet not reproach from thee affection fears.
In anguish comforted and want sufficed
Thy spirit joy'd on earth, as now with Christ.

EPITAPH ON R. H., IN DERRY CATHEDRAL.

Down through our crowded lanes, and closer air,
O friend, how beautiful thy footsteps were;
When through the fever's waves of fire they trod,
A form was with thee like the son of God.
'Twas but one step for those victorious feet,
From their day's walk unto the golden street;
And they who watch'd that walk, so bright and brief,
Have mark'd this marble with their hope and grief

INSCRIPTION

O in the quiet haven, safe for aye,
If lost to us in port one stormy day,
Borne with a public pomp by just decree,
Heroic sailor ! from that fatal sea,
A city vows this marble unto thee.
And here, in this calm place, where never din
Of earth's great waterfloods shall enter in,
Where to our human hearts two thoughts are given—
One Christ's self-sacrifice, the other Heaven,—
Here is it meet for grief and love to grave
The Christ-taught bravery that died to save,
The life not lost, but found beneath the wave.

III.

WITHERED LAUREL LEAVES.

ODE

ADDRESSED TO THE EARL OF DERBY, AND RECITED IN THE SHELDO-
NIAN THEATRE, OXFORD, AT HIS INSTALLATION AS CHANCELLOR
OF THE UNIVERSITY, JUNE 1, 1853.

I HAD been thinking of the antique masque
  Before high peers and peeresses at Court,
Of the strong gracefulness of Milton's task,
  "Rare Ben's" gigantic sport—

Those delicate creations, full of strange
  And perilous stuff, wherein the silver flood
And crownèd city suffer'd human change
  Like things of flesh and blood.

And I was longing for a hand like those
  Somewhere in bower of learning's fine retreat,
That it might fling immortally one rose,
  At Stanley's honour'd feet.

Fair as that woman whom the Prophet old
  In Ardath * met, lamenting for her dead,
With sackcloth cast above the tiar of gold,
  And ashes on her head.

* 2 Esdras ix. 38.

Methought I met a lady yester-even ;
   A passionless grief, that had nor tear nor wail,
Sat on her pure proud face, that gleam'd to Heaven,
   White as a moonlit sail.

She spake.   "On this pale brow are looks of youth,
   Yet angels, listening on the argent floor,
Know that these lips have been proclaiming truth
   Nine hundred years and more.

"And Isis knows what time-grey towers rear'd up,
   Gardens and groves and cloister'd halls are mine,
Where quaff my sons from many a myrrhine cup
   Draughts of ambrosial wine.

"He knows how night by night my lamps are lit,
   How day by day my bells are ringing clear,
Mother of ancient lore, and Attic wit,
   And discipline severe.

"It may be long ago my dizzied brain,
   Enchanted swam beneath Rome's master spell,
Till like light tinctured by the painted pane
   Thought in *her* colours fell.

"Yet when the great old tongue with strong effect
   Woke from its sepulchre across the sea,
The subtler spell of Grecian intellect
   Work'd mightily in me.

"Time pass'd—my groves were full of warlike stirs ;
   The student's heart was with the merry spears,
Or keeping measure to the clanking spurs
   Of Rupert's Cavaliers.

" All those long ages, like a holy mother,
   I rear'd my children to a lore sublime,
Picking up fairer shells than any other
   Along the shores of Time.

" And must I speak at last of sensual sleep,
   The dull forgetfulness of aimless years?
Oh, let me turn away my head, and weep
   Than Rachel's bitterer tears—

" Tears for the passionate hearts I might have won,
   Tears for the age with which I might have striven,
Tears for a hundred years of work undone,
   Crying like blood to Heaven.

" I have repented—and my glorious name
   Stands scutcheon'd round with blazonry more bright.
The wither'd rod, the emblem of my shame,
   Bloom'd blossoms in a night.

" And I have led my children on steep mountains,
   By fine attraction of my spirit brought
Up to the dark inexplicable fountains
   That are the springs of thought,—

" Led them, where on the old poetic shore
   The flowers that change not with the changing moon
Breathe round young hearts, as breathes the sycamore
   About the bees in June.

" And I will bear them, as on eagle wings,
   To leave them bow'd before the sapphire throne,
High o'er the haunts where dying pleasure sings
   With sweet and swanlike tone.

o

"And I will lead the ages great expansions,
  Progressive circles toward thought's Sabbath rest,
And point beyond them to the many mansions
  Where Christ is with the blest.

"Am I not pledged who gave my bridal ring
  To that old man heroic, strong, and true,
Whose grey-hair'd virtue was a nobler thing
  Than even Waterloo?

"Surely that spousal morn my chosen ones
  Felt their hearts moving to mysterious calls,
And the old pictures of my sainted sons
  Look'd brighter from the walls.

"He sleeps at last—no wind's tempestuous breath
  Play'd a dead march upon the moaning billow,
What time God's angel visited with death
  The old Field Marshal's pillow.

"There was no omen of a great disaster
  Where castled Walmer stands beside the shore;
The evening clouds, like pillar'd alabaster,
  Hung huge and silent o'er.

"The moon in brightness walk'd the fleecy rack,
  Walk'd up and down among the starry fires;
Heaven's great cathedral was not hung with black
  Up to its topmost spires.

"But mine own Isis kept a solemn chiming,
  A silver requiescat all night long,
And mine old trees with all their leaves were timing
  The sorrow of the song.

" And through mine angel-haunted aisles of beauty
  From the grand organs gush'd a music dim,
Lauds for a champion who had done his duty,
  I knew they were for *him !*

" But night is fading—I must deck my hair
  For the high pageant of the gladsome morn ;
I would not meet my chosen Stanley there
  In sorrow, or in scorn.

" I know him nobler than his noble blood,
  Seeking for wisdom as the earth's best pearl,
And bring my brightest jewelry to stud
  The baldrick of mine Earl.

" I, and my children, with our fairest gift,
  With song will meet him, and with music's swell :
The coronal a king might love to lift,
  It will beseem him well.

" And when the influx of the perilous fight
  Shall be around us as a troubled sea,
He will remember, like a red cross knight,
  God, and this day, and me."

THE DEATH OF JACOB.*

Ἅτινά ἐστιν ἀλληγορούμενα.

I READ how Israel, after life's long lent,
    Enter'd the quiet Easter-Eve of Faith.
We do thee grievous wrong, O eloquent,
    And just and mighty Death !

Life is a cave,† where shadows gleam and glide
    Between our dim eyes and a distant light ;
Faint breaks the booming of the outer tide,
    Faint falls its line of white.

When in the cave our spirits darkling stand,
    Where the light strangely flickers on the floor,
Comes death, and softly leads us by the hand
    Unto the cavern door.

I saw the Syrian sunset's meteor crown
    Hang over Bethel for a little space ;
I saw a gentle wanderer lie down
    With tears upon his face.

* Being the Poem to which an Accessit was awarded by the judges of the best Poem on a Sacred Subject, in the University of Oxford, June 1, 1857.

† Ἴδε γὰρ ἀνθρώπους οἷον ἐν καταγείῳ οἰκήσει σπηλαιώδει . . . φῶς δὲ αὐτοῖς πυρὸς ἀνῶθεν καὶ πόῤῥωθεν καὀμενον ὄπισθεν αὐτῶν, κ.τ.λ. (Plat.)

Sheer up the fathomless, transparent blue,
  Rose jasper battlement, and crystal wall;
Rung all the night air, piercèd through and through
    With songs angelical.

And a great ladder was set up the while
  From earth to heaven, with angels on each round,
Barks that bore precious freight to earth's far isle,
    Or sail'd back homeward bound.

Ah ! many a time we look, on starlit nights,
  Up to the sky as Jacob did of old,
Look longing up to the eternal lights
    To spell their lines of gold;

But nevermore, as to the Hebrew lone,
  Each on his way the angels walk abroad;
And nevermore we hear with audible tone
    The awful voice of God.

Yet, to pure eyes, the ladder still is set,
  And angel visitants still come and go;
Many bright messengers are moving yet
    From this dark world below.

Thoughts, that are surely Faith's outspreading wings;
  Prayers of the Church, aye keeping time and tryst;
Heart-wishes, making bee-like murmurings,
    Their flower the Eucharist;

Spirits elect, through suffering render'd meet
  For those high mansions ; from the nursery door,
Bright babes that climb up with their clay-cold feet
    Unto the golden floor ;—

These are the messengers, for ever wending
　　From earth to Heaven, that faith alone may scan ;
These are the angels of our God, ascending
　　Upon the Son of Man.*

I saw a tent beside the lotos river ;
　　I saw an old man bow'd upon his bed ;
Methought the river sang, "I roll for ever,
　　But he will soon be dead.

"Long since, his grandsire walk'd beside my stream ;
　　His wife, a lily, lit my lilied meadows : †
Long since they glided, like a magic dream,
　　Into the old world shadows.

"Up where his grandsire rests the mummy goes,
　　Up to the shrivell'd lily's mask of clay,—
But on my rolling music grandly flows,
　　And it shall flow for aye !"

Whereto another voice kept chanting on,
　　"The shadows come, the shadows go, old river !
But when thy music shall be mute and gone,
　　He shall sing psalms for ever."

And then methought, beside that pastoral tent,
　　The ladder rose from the green land below ;
Fair spiritual creatures made descent,
　　And beckon'd him to go.

* St. John i. 51. "The disciples could not but think of the ladder of Heaven at Bethel, when our Lord uttered these well-known words." (Stier's "Words of Jesus.") The words ἀπ' ἄρτι ὄψεσθε must be understood of the abiding continuous vision of faith, not of any momentary manifestation.

† "Abraham went down to sojourn in Egypt. . . . When Abraham was come into Egypt, the Egyptians beheld the woman that she was very fair." (Gen. xii. 10, 14.)

But up the stream of days he seem'd to float,
  And twice seven years was toiling for his wife;
And all his thought lay heaving like a boat
  On the long swell of life.

How statuelike that shape in shadows deep—
  Like one of marble in the minster's rest,
With a pale babe—not dead, but gone to sleep
  For ever on her breast.

And the white mother's breast may seem to heave,
  And the white babe to feel about her face;
'Tis but our restless hearts that thus deceive
  The quiet of the place.

And Rachel look'd upon her Israel,—wann'd
  Like a white flower with the summer rain,
So she with sweat of child-birth,—her thin hand
  Laid on the counterpane.

Near Ephrath there's a pillar'd tomb apart;
  It throws a shadow on her where she lies—
And she, a shadow on her husband's heart,
  Of household memories.

Then by the death-bed two fair boys bent down—
  So bend two wild flowers where the dark firs rise.
Fell first upon the younger's golden crown
  Faith's blessing sunlight-wise. *

* "And Israel stretched out his right hand, and laid it upon Ephraim's head, who was the younger, . . . guiding his hands wittingly." (Gen. xlviii. 14.)

"By faith Jacob, when he was a dying, blessed both the sons of Joseph." (Heb. xi. 21.)

Gather yourselves together, hear ye well,
    Your fair adventure from the lips of death !
Gather yourselves, ye sons of Israel !
    Hear what in song he saith ; *

That so the old men, in the after times,
    May find the wingèd words by memory sought ;
Tracing the golden feathers of their rhymes
    Through the thick leaves of thought.†

Darkly, O Reuben, doth the tower of Edar
    Hang down its heavy shadow on the lea ;
Dark droops the shadow of the mountain cedar ;
    Dark droops thy deed o'er thee.‡

With him, O brothers of the bloody hand !
    Hard by the lustful heart dwell hearts of hate !
Be ye left lone and scatter'd in the land,
    Who left love desolate.§

Sweet ring the merry tabret and the pipe
    On Judah's mountains all the vintage long,
From the first flower, until the grape is ripe,
    Soundeth a pleasant song.

---

* Gen. xlix. 1–2.

† See Hengstenberg's answer to the objections to Jacob's prophecy arising from its poetical character, and proving that the difficulty of handing down such a composition was diminished by its metrical cast. ("Christologes," lxviii. 70.)

‡ Gen. xlix. 4.—"And Israel spread his tent beyond the tower of Edar ; and when Israel dwelt in that land, Reuben went and lay with Bilhah his father's concubine." (Gen. xxxv. 21, 22.)

§ And they slew Hamor and Shechem . . . with the edge of the sword, and took Dinah out of of Shechem's house." (Gen. xxxiv. 26.)

Whelp of the lion, thee thy brethren praise,
    The weir wolf couches at thy kingly feet,
The hissing of the serpent guards thy ways *
    Where horse and horsemen meet.

Old lion of the hills, the Heavens assign
    Rule unto thee, and law, and high estate,
Till Shiloh come forth of the lion line,
    On whom the nations wait.

Through all thy waters lift a battle shout,
    Shout forth, O Jordan, for a warrior comes ;†
Dark forests, roll your stormy music out,
    Like a long roll of drums.

Clash all your boughs, like shields that shock and sound,
    Where, with his shield and buckler, Gad appears ;
Lift your tall stems like sheaves of lances, bound
    Over his plump of spears.

From Joseph's blossom'd valleys sail abroad
    The pale blue vapours born of living rills ; ‡
From his high head are seen the stars of God
    Crowning the eternal hills.

And the white tents of Issachar are spread,
    Couch'd in good rest the craven fears each comer ; §
In sooth a pleasant land of drowsy-head
    Lit by the sleepy summer.

* Alluding to the geographical position of Benjamin, "ravening as a wolf," and Dan, "a serpent by the way, biting horse's heels."

† For indications of the warlike character of the tribe of Gad, see 1 Chron. v. 18 ; xii. 8.

‡ See Lieutenant Van de Velde's account of the vapours in the vale of Shechem, which render the scenery so peculiar.

§ The sluggish and unwarlike character of the tribe of Issachar is amply illustrated by its subsequent history.

Asher is grey with many an olive-tree,
  And Napthali puts forth his goodly boughs.*
Seen from the shore, Zebulon's silver sea
    Shines round Zidonian prows.

Hush'd is the song, the tribesmen all are bless'd,
  According to his blessing, every one ;
But still the old man's spirit may not rest
    Until he charge each son—

Not where the Pharaohs lie, with incense breath'd
  Round awful galleries, grim with shapes of wrath,
Hawk-headed, vulture-pinion'd, serpent-wreath'd,
    Hued like an Indian moth—

But lay him where, from forest or green slope
  To Mamre's cave, the low wind breatheth balm,
Chanteth a litany of immortal hope,
    Singeth a funeral psalm.

Then slowly upward did the cold death creep
  From foot and face with its strange lines of white,
Like foam-streaks on a river, dark and deep,
    Lash'd by the winds all night.

And then the feet were gather'd in the bed,
  The silver stairs were all astir with wings—
Whatever lauds are sweetly sung, or said,
    Or struck on plausive strings,

Whatever harmony conch or trumpet rolls,
  From angels swell'd, address'd to entertain
With gratulation high those purgèd souls
    For which the Lamb was slain.

* Such seems to be the more probable rendering of Gen. xlix. 21.

We die—but no unearthly breezes bless,
  Blown from futurity, the parting soul—
Through tangled mazes of our consciousness
    No prophet-sunlights roll ;

Yet as what time the softly floating mist
  Hangs o'er the hush'd sea and the leafy land,
Nature, a passionate pale evangelist,
    Takes pen and scroll in hand,

And, looking upward, writes beneath the sea
  A colourless story, beautiful but dim :
So Jacob saw the Lord in mystery,
    And darkly sang of Him.

But unto us He comes in fuller light,
  His pale and dying lips with woe foredone—
No need to seek, through many a day and night,
    By starlight for the sun !

So come, O Shiloh ! with the thorn-crown'd head ;
  Come, with the fountain flowing forth abroad ;
Bring faith the sacred Eucharistic bread,
    Give her the wine of God.

Come, with the open'd arms for sin to see
  The sacramental side for sinners riven.
Oh, in the hour of death we climb by Thee
    Up to the gate of Heaven !

Like a tall ship that beareth slow and proud
  A fallen chief—for pall and plume in motion
The death-dark top-mast and the death-white shroud
    Drift o'er the silver ocean.

Silent the helmsman stands beside the wheel,
　　Silent the mariners in their watches wait,
And a great music rolls before the keel
　　As through an abbey gate :

Like that tall ship a grand procession comes *
　　Up from old Father Nile to Hebron's hill ;
But no dead march is beat upon the drums,
　　And every trump is still.

Heartsore, and footsore with the march of life—
　　Soldier of God, whose fields were foughten well—
Resteth him from the cumbrance and the strife
　　World-wearied Israel.

Twelve harps of life are round that unstrung lyre,
　　Twelve living flowers are round that wither'd one,
Twelve clouds with his red sunset all on fire
　　Are round that sunken sun.

Those twelve brave hearts are tolling evermore,
　　For every heart beats like a muffled bell,
And still they ring, " Thy march of life is o'er—
　　O weary soul, rest well."

Still it sails onward, where the Red Sea fills
　　With snowy drift of shells his coral bowers,
On through the wondrous land of rose-red hills
　　To that of rose-red flowers : †

---

　　* " And Joseph went up to bury his father, . . . and there went up
with him both chariots and horsemen : and it was a very great
company." (Gen. l. 7–9.)
　　† Dean Stanley compares the shells of the Red Sea to bleaching
bones, or white porcelain. " The mountains of the Sinaitic peninsula
were described by Diodorus Siculus, as of a bright scarlet hue ; viewed

The land where aye, through many a purple gap,
　　The wanderer sees a mountain wall upspring,
And ever in his ear the wild waves flap
　　　　Like a great eagle's wing;

Meet battlement for the race that dwells alone,
　　Music to match, monotonous and grave,
The tongue, whose dark old words are all its own,
　　　　Pure as the mid-sea wave.*

Ever I walk with that funereal train—
　　The stars shine over it for tapers tall,
And Jordan's music is the requiem strain
　　　　Drawn out from fall to fall.

Come, O thou south wind! with thy fragrance faint,
　　Bring from those folded forests, on thy breath,
Balm for the mummy, lying like a saint,
　　　　Upon his car of death.†

Bear him, ye bearers! lay him down at last
　　In still Machpelah, down by Leah's side—
On that pale bridegroom shimmering is cast,
　　　　Laid by that awful bride.

Rests he not well whose pilgrim staff and shoon ‡
　　Lie in his tent—for through the golden street §

even in the soberest light, it gives a richness to the landscape " (p. 11).
For the profusion of scarlet flowers characteristic of Palestine, see *ibid.*,
p. 138.

　* Capientur signa haud levia de ingreniis populorum ex linguis
ipsorum. Hebræi verbis tam paucis et minimè commistis utuntur, ut
plane ex lingua ipsa quis perspiciat gentem fuisse illam Nazaræam, et
a reliquis gentibus separatam. (Bacon, "De Aug. Scien.," lib. vi. ch. 1.)

　† " The Physicians embalmed Israel." (Gen. l. 2.)

　‡ Gen. xlvii. 9; Heb. xi. 13.　　　　　　§ Heb. xi. 10.

They walk, and stumble not, on roads star-strewn,
    With their unsandall'd feet?

Rests he not well who keepeth watch and ward,
    In sweet possession of the land loved most,
Till, marshall'd by the Angel of the Lord,
        Shall come the Heaven-sent host?

Who has not felt, within some churchyard spot,
    When evening's pencil shades the pale-gold sky,
" Here, at the closing of my life's calm lot,
        Here would I love to lie?

" Here, where the poet thrush so often pours
    His requiem, hidden in green aisles of lime,
And, bloody red along the sycamores,
        Creepeth the summer-time;

" Where through the ruin'd church's broken walls
    Glimmers all night the vast and solemn sea,
As through our broken hopes the brightness shines,
        Of our eternity."

But when we die, we rest, far, far away;
    Not over us the lime-trees lift their bowers,
And the young sycamores their shadows sway
        O'er graves that are not ours.

Yet he is happy, wheresoe'er he lie,
    Round whom the purple calms of Eden spread;
Who sees his Saviour with the heart's pure eye,*
        He is the happy dead!

* Πεφωτισμένους τοὺς ὀφθαλμοὺς τῆς καρδίας.   (Eph. i. 18.)

By the rough brook of life no more he wrestles,
    Huddling its hoarse waves until night depart;
No more the pale face of a Rachel nestles
    Upon his broken heart.

He is encircled by the quiet home,
    From whose safe hold no little lamb is lost;
The Jegar-sahadutha of the tomb *
    No Laban ever crost!

I saw again.   Behold! Heaven's open door; †
    Behold! a throne—the Seraphim stood o'er it;
The white-robed Elders fell upon the floor,
    And flung their crowns before it.

I saw a wondrous book; an Angel strong ‡
    To heaven and earth proclaim'd his loud appeals:
But a hush pass'd across the seraph's song,
    For none might loose the seals.

Then fast as rain to death-cry of the year,
    Tears of St. John to that sad cry were given— §
It was a wondrous thing to see a tear
    Fall on the floor of Heaven.

And a sweet voice said, "Weep not: wherefore fails,
    Eagle of God, thy heart, the high and leal?
The Lion out of Judah's tribe prevails
    To loose the sevenfold seal."

---

* "And Laban called it Jegar-sahadutha. . . . This heap be witness that I will not pass over this heap to thee for harm." (Gen. xxxi. 47, 52.)

† Apoc. iv.

‡ "I saw a strong angel proclaiming with a loud voice." (Apoc. v. 2.)

§ "And I wept much." (Apoc. v. 4.)

'Twas Israel's voice; and straightway, up above,*
　Stood in the midst a wondrous Lamb, snow white,†
Heart-wounded with the deep sweet wounds of love,‡
　　Eternal, Infinite.

Then rose the song no ear had heard before;
　Then from the white-robed throng high anthem woke;
And fast as spring-tide on the sealess shore,
　　The Hallelujahs broke.

Who dreams of God when passionate youth is high,
　When first life's weary waste his feet have trod,—
Who seeth angels' footfalls in the sky,
　　Working the work of God,—

His sun shall fade as gently as it rose;
　Through the dark woof of death's approaching night
His faith shall shoot, at life's prophetic close,‖
　　Some threads of golden light;

For him the silver ladder shall be set—
　His Saviour shall receive his latest breath.—
He walketh to a fadeless coronet,
　　Up through the gate of death.

---

* "And one of the elders said unto me, Weep not," etc.　"Videtur esse Patriarcha Jacobus, quia ex ipsius vaticinio Christo nomen leonis tribuitur." (*cf.* Bengel, *in loco.*)

† Apoc. v. 6.

‡ "Grande et suave vulnus amoris." (Bernard in Cant.)

‖ "These all died in faith." (Heb. xi. 13.) "Fides maximè apud morientes viget."

THE WATERS OF BABYLON.*

"C'est là le mystère après lequel soupirent toutes les âmes exilées, qui
s'affligent sur les fleuves de Babylon en se souvenant de Sion."

A DREAM of many waters.   I beheld,
And lo ! a summer night in Babylon,
And the great river, even Euphrates, wash'd
The land of Shinar, somewhat swifter now,
When snows were melting on the Armenian hills.
So by the hundred gates, lintel and post
All polish'd brass, the waves went washing on.
And on the flood the osier barges rode,
Shield-shaped, with earthen jars of palm-tree wine
Heap'd on the deck, and dark shapes stretch'd around.
League upon league, through tracts of wheat and corn,
That look'd on boundless plains, like knightly hosts,
Far glimmering with pale and ghostly gold ;
Through ranks of cedar, planted by the Lord,
Round the lign-aloes by the river side,
Had they dropp'd down the flood.   Then the tilth ceased,
And banks, like mountains, rose on either hand,
Worthy of wonderment, the work of kings ;

* Oxford University Prize Poem on a Sacred Subject, 1857-1860.

And long canals stretch'd, lighted by the moon
And by the company of Chaldean stars ;
Till there came houses, bastion'd fortresses,
With lion gonfalons, and a maze of streets.
I saw the terraced pyramid of Bel ;
And a vast palace with its gardens hung
As by art-magic in the spicèd air,
Pencill'd like purple islands fast asleep.
But evermore—by all the gates of brass,
And where the barges floated down the stream,
And far along the sloping line of streets
Hung with a thousand cressets naphtha-lit,
And up among the garden terraces—
I heard the murmur of Euphrates' flood.

So as I linger'd there, anon methought
The tide of life in that great city pent
Parted in twain and took its separate way.
For one moved upward by the basalt wall :
A host of fierce-eyed men with long black hair
Stream'd o'er white tunics, their dark faces wreath'd
With turbans white, in every hand a staff
Carven with lilies or with eagle head.
And haughty girls in gilded cars swept on
To the Assyrian Aphrodites' fane,
With faces passion-flush'd or terror-pale,—
Red and white roses rich, but soon to fade.
High on the palace terraces above,
There walk'd a king *—it made me fear to see
How like he was to those old sculptured kings,
Black-curl'd, black-bearded, full of state and woe,
Who sit the world out on their chairs of stone,
Staring for ever on the arrow-heads,

* Dan. iv. 29.

Wherein their bloody chronicles are writ.
There, too, I saw grey-beard astrologers,
Who read the silver horologue of heaven;
And them who shape the purpose shadow'd forth
In visions of the head upon the bed;
And priests who give attendance at the shrine
Well strewn, that hath no image of its God,
Or at that other where he sits eterne,
Statue, and throne, and pedestal of gold,
Grinning and glimmering thro' the frankincense.

From all these diverse went another way
Another concourse gentler of regard.
And as a widow, when her son is dead,
Putteth her white lip down to the white shroud,
And communeth a little while with death,
So did the exiles commune with their past.
Psalms did they murmur—poesy of him,
Shepherd, king, saint, and penitent, who wore
The golden grief that gave the golden song :—
And later lamentations.   For as when
A wandering man, beside an ocean shore
Belated, hears the waves upon the beach
Discoursing drearily, and night hangs black
On the black rocks, over the moaning sea ;—
But suddenly there circles in the gloom
A bird's voice wailing, like a soul in pain,
Not dispossess'd of some immortal hope :
So Jeremiah wailed o'er Judah's path,
Still round and round that strange old alphabet
Weaving his long funereal chant of woe,
Still singing sweetly of the seventy years !

I saw the exiles seek the river side,
There where the willows grey grew in the midst
Of Babylon, and hang their harps thereon.

Thus evermore in ear of either throng
Sounded the voice of waters.   It went up
Over the city, where the forests hang,
Sleepily parleying in the charmèd light
Round alabaster stairs and curious flowers
From Media brought, and sunny steeps of Ind.
How different to each !—To these it swept
On with a din of Oriental war.
It sounded an alarm that wakened up
Far echoes from far rivers all night long,
Angering the dragon in his lotos-bed,
And bringing Persian kings unto the brink
Of the Choaspes with their silver jars.
Like a soothsayer it denounced a woe
On Tigris, telling the predestined time
When he should wail along a waste of bricks
Painted with pine-cones and colossal bulls.
And like a divination it aroused
As it were gods ascending from the earth,
Disquieting old kings to bring them up,
Urukh and Ilgi, Iva, and the rest,
Whose politic alliances, fierce wars,
And love and hate have perished like themselves,
Forgotten in the city where they dwelt.

But to the other throng the river told
Things written in their great old Hebrew book.
It told how it had swept through Eden once,
A bright chord of the fourfold river-lyre.
And it had old-world songs of Abraham,

And him of Rehoboth who went to rule
Among the dark-eyed dukes on Seir's red rocks,*
And him of Pethor,† walking wrapped in thought.
Anon it seem'd to sing : " My waves flow past
A dungeon, and one bound with chains of brass,
A king, a crownless, childless, eyeless ghost ! ‡
And on my surface lights and shadows play,
And moonlights quiver on the ripply lines,
The silver roll among my sighing reeds,
And the stars look into my silent depths,
But on the awful river of his thoughts,
Black as the waters of a mountain lake
What time the hills are powder'd white with snow,
Sunlight, and moon, and stars, are not at all :
Dark, dark, all draped with shadows of his life."

Then came another tale—a legend wild—
How the Ten Tribes, the banish'd of the Lord
Took counsel with themselves, that they would leave
The multitude of heathen, and fare forth
To a far country where there never came
Oarsman or sail.   A penitential host,
They enter'd the Euphrates by the ford.
And often hath the moon at midnight hung
Pillars of luminous silver o'er the wave,
But not a pillar half so broad and bright
As that which steer'd them on while the Most High
Held still the flood.   And aye their way they took
Twice nine long months, until they reach'd the land
Arsareth.§   There the mountains gird them in ;

---

* Gen. xxxvi. 19, 31, 37.   † Num. xxii. 5.
‡ Zedekiah—2 Kings xxv. 7.
§ See legend of the journey of the Ten Tribes across Euphrates to
Arsareth in 2 Esdras.

And o'er the gleaming granite pass white clouds,
That sail from awful waterfalls, and catch
And tear their silver fleeces on the pines.
And never hunter scaled those granite peaks,
And never wandering man hath heard the roar
Of cataracts soften'd through those folds of fir,
But a great temple hangs upon the hills.
And ever and anon rolls through its gates
A mighty music, washing through the pines,
And silver trumps still snarl at the new moon ;
And all their life is sacrament, and psalm,
Vesper, or festival, and holy deed.
There do they dwell until the latter time,
When God Most High shall stay the springs again.

The waters changed their meaning.   There came down
Some of the others to Euphrates' brink,
And much they question'd why those harps hung there.
Saying, " Come, sing us one of Sion's songs ! "
How shall they sing God's song in the strange land ?
For it is native of the Temple, laid
Like a white flower on Moriah's breast ;
And it is not for Asia's sealike plain,
But for the shadows of the purple hills ;
Not for the broad and even-pulsing stream,
But for the land where Jordan passioneth
His poetry of waterfalls night and day,
Anger'd by cataracts, lull'd by nightingales,
Crown'd with white foam, and triumphing for ever,
That is to the Euphrates, as a saint
Full of sweet yearnings and of tears divine
Is to some cold and passionless idol god,
Imprison'd in its rigid marble lines.

Next, as from a far country, there came one.[*]
Slow was his gait, his garment travel-stain'd,
And in his hand methought he held a scroll,
Written from right to left Semitic-wise.
Then one said to him, " Wherefore art thou come ? "
And he, " I come from him of Anathoth."
Whereat he bound a stone upon the scroll,
And flung it far away into the flood;
When suddenly a trumpet-blast wax'd loud
Against Chaldea, rousing Ararat,
And Ashkenaz and Minni, kingdoms old.
Yea, instantaneously a mighty voice
Of Heaven, and earth, and all that is therein,
Sang over Babylon.   And as far north
The ice-bound mariner looks up, and lo !
The sky is spann'd with the auroral arch,
And the Heav'n, full of glory, blossometh
With light unspeakable : so now, methought,
The sky grew radiant up above my head,
World upon world.   And then I heard a song,
Angels, archangels, and the company,
Of Heav'n chanting unto golden harps
With exultation—" Babylon the great
Is fallen, fallen "—and from earth below
Rose echo, " Fallen, fallen," back again.
Whereon I thought that I could hear far off
The cedars and the firs of Lebanon,[†]
With a wind rustling all their odorous robes,
That shaped itself in long low syllables,
As if a happy thought went sighing through
Their dark green halls and sombre colonnades,
Saying, " No feller comes against us now,

[*] Seraiah—Jer. li. 59.   [†] Isaiah xiv.

Since they have laid thee low, O Babylon!"
And the great river sobb'd, "O Babylon!"
I beheld gods, and demigods, and kings,
Like shadows upon unsubstantial thrones.
I saw the crowns upon their wither'd brows,
Like the thin circlet of the waning moon
Over a thin white cloud.   Ranged were they all,
A royal consistory, row on row,
Sleeping their sleep.   But now their ranks were stirred,
As the wan leaves, shrunken from red to white,
—The chestnuts' ashes, or the beeches' fire—
Are stirr'd in heaps, and a shrill murmuring went
Among them, like the wailing of the birds.
And they look'd narrowly on one that came
Into their company, and laugh'd, and said,
" How art thou fallen, O thou Morning star!
For we are kings at least, and take our fill
Of rest, each one in glory on his bed,
Strewn with sweet odours, divers kinds of spice.
But thou art as a wanderer in our land,
Thy carcase trodden under foot of men—
Disrobed, disscepted, dropp'd with blood, discrown'd!"
Then Heav'n and the abyss were mute once more,
And the curse fell upon broad walls, high gates,
Utterly broken, burnèd in the fire:
And the curse fell on garden-terraces,
Faded, all faded, like a golden cloud,
And tumbled like a cliff in heaps of stones;
And the curse fell upon Euphrates last,
Fountain and flood and all his sea dried up.

Yet other shapes and sounds came to me still.
I saw a fire dark-red in the fierce sky,
Three shadowy figures flitting to and fro;

Far off I heard their *Benedicite.* *
I saw a host, across the river's bed,
Trample right onward to a palace-gate,
Whence from a great feast fled a thousand lords,
And dark sultanas dress'd in white symars.
And in the hall I saw a blaze of light
Round gold and silver cups of strange device,
And one mysterious figure, scarlet-robed,†
Waiting unmoved, and on the daïs high
A king, the wine still red on his white lips.
And I beheld a barge upon the wave ;
Lo ! at its helm there was a godlike form,‡
A glittering tiar above his kausia.
Sitting the centre of a light of gems,
Shadow'd by silk-embroider'd sails, he steered
His pinnace to the dyke Pallakopas,
Keeping his royal court and state on deck,
As his yacht bore him to see the pictured graves
Of the old kings, that sleep world without end,
Where shadows are the only moving things.
And one kept court upon the deck as well,
White-lipp'd, and grim, and stern, and that was Death.
And next a stately chamber, muffled round
With golden curtains, rose beside the stream :
And, his face cover'd with a silken veil,
Walked the Resch Glutha§ among agèd men,
Thin faces, pinch'd-up foreheads, narrow hearts,
Whereon the thoughts of God's eternal book
Are stamp'd in petty legendary lore,
As the great waves with all their noble beat

* The Song of the Three Children. † Dan. v. 29.
‡ Alexander the Great. See Grote, "History," vol. xii.
§ The "Chief of the Captivity" among the Babylonian Jews. The Gemara, Mischna, and Talmud grew up in Babylon.

Carve out those feather'd lines along the strand
And last I thought Euphrates was dried up,
And o'er his bed the kings of the Orient,
Surging with war's full stream of clanging gold,*
March'd to the battle of Almighty God.

But on before me swept the moonlit stream
That had entranced me with its memories—
A thousand battles, and one burst of Psalms,
Rolling his waters to the Indian Sea
Beyond Balsara and Elana far,
Nigh to two thousand miles from Ararat.
And his full music took a finer tone,
And sang me something of a " gentler stream " †
That rolls for ever to another shore
Whereof our God Himself is the sole sea.
And Christ's dear love the pulsing of the tide,
And His sweet Spirit is the breathing wind.
Something it chanted, too, of exiled men
On the sad bank of that strange river Life,
Hanging the harp of their deep heart desires
To rest upon the willow of the Cross,
And longing for the everlasting hills,
Mount Sion, and Jerusalem of God.
And then I thought I knelt, and kneeling heard
Nothing—save only the long wash of waves,
And one sweet psalm that sobbed for evermore.

* Πολλῷ ῥευμάτι—χρυσοῦ καναχῆς. (Soph., " Antig.," 130.)
  † " A gentler stream with gladness still
        The city of our God shall fill." (Psa. xlvi. 4.)

ISHMAEL.[*]

An angel's voice—and lo ! on Hagar's ears,
   Sitting in Zophar by the well forlorn,
   Four words—the future of a life unborn ;
Four words—the story of four thousand years !

Here in this West, the land of onward wills,
   Our restless history moves, and all things change ;
   But there they stand unmoved, as is the range
And steadfast front of the eternal hills.

And as the man for ever, so the race,
   Wearing about it through the changeless years
   The self-same laughters and the self-same tears,
The self-same lights, and shadows on the face !

So Ishmael yet can rein his battle steeds
   Over the burning stretches vast and wide,
   The country from the Red Sea's western side
To where Euphrates moans among his reeds ;

Then back and back, o'er miles of desert sand,
   Till over-wearied horse and rider rest
   Beneath some Pyramid, whose lofty crest
Welcomes them nobly to their mother-land.

[*] This poem, by my son, was awarded the prize for the best Poem on a Sacred Subject in the University of Oxford, 1875-1878.

Shall there be music for them ? any cry ?
  Yes ! Memnon, rousing when the dawn is near,
  Shall wake a strain so desolate and drear,
It suits the wanderer's children riding by.

A race not wholly cursed, not wholly blest,
  Countless as sands—into the desert vast
  Plump after plump of spears before me past,
Seeking, it seem'd in vain, for any rest.

I thought the centuries were rolling back,
  And those wild horsemen as they rode apace
  'Might meet the wandering father of their race,
And comfort Hagar on her lonely track ;

And they might come ere the quick evening fell—
  Future and past together strangely met,—
  And find the mother, and with lips still wet
The boy reviving by that charmèd well.

Round them a space of yellow sand unroll'd
  Lies weltering in the evening's purple light—
  His heritage and theirs—before the night
Sweeps the red sunlight from that cloth of gold.

Vain fancy ; for no thought the poet weaves,
  Clothing his figures with a mortal toil,
  Can add aught nobler,—nay would rather spoil
The simple truth on God's immortal leaves,

Which, undestroy'd, lives on divinely yet.
  For whensoe'er an Ishmael is born,
  Then are the lips of Hagar wreath'd in scorn,
And Sarah's bitter heart cannot forget.

Oh, the poor mother that was never wife !
  The twice-pathetic anguish of the slave ;
  Turning away from that she could not save,
Fainting so fast beside the streams of life.*

Yet her wild son some earthly blessing wins—
  Children, the earnest of a countless race,
  With sunrise on the dying archer's face,
Fallen amid his twelve stout Paladins : †

And reconciliation, it may be,
  When to the silence of Machpelah's cave,
  Owning the greatness of the truce death gave,
Isaac and Ishmael came heavily,

To lay their father in his rocky bed.‡
  How should they not put all contention by !
  He found it such a gentle thing to die—
And there is peace amid the mighty dead.

There let them linger for a little while—
  Those brothers sunder'd long and far away,—
  Merging in sacred tears, what space they may,
The heavenly laughter and the mocking smile.

So that old story—mingled joy and strife,
  Divine and human—through a mist of tears
  Speaks to men's hearts across a sea of years,
True as the imperfections of our life.

* Genesis xvi. 14.   † Genesis xxv. 16.
‡ "His sons Isaac and Ishmael buried him in the cave of Machpelah."
(Gen. xxv. 9.)

Its streams shall fail not, for in every clime
    Hagars and Ishmaels of years to be,
    Lifting up sudden eyes of hope, shall see
The fountain love amid the sands of time ;

And God be with them, coming as He came—
    Not Isaac's only, but the Lord of all ;
    Softly on overburden'd hearts shall fall
The music of His universal Name.*

Short glimpse of heaven, and brief respite from pain ;
    For all the future, with its heavy cost
    Of progress unattain'd, and blessings lost,
Of tears and triumphs, calls us back again.

Thou shalt not set thy city on a hill,
    There to hold festival, and royal state,
    Girdled with walls, and buckled with a gate,
And fondly thinking to abide there still,—

Like some grey king, upon his head a crown,
    Dreaming in some grey castle, unaware
    Of Time's fell feet upon the marble stair,
Stealing right on to shake his greatness down.

Thou, too, art but a mortal ! yet thy roof
    Is builded up of air, and lit with stars ;
    Thy pillars are the fluted sunrise bars,
Thy walls of rock are time and tempest-proof.

There thou shalt dwell, in more than kingly power,
    Beneath some palm ; and when the hills show brown
    At even, with the shadows bowing down,
Shalt bow and worship in that holy hour.

* " Elohim " (Gen. xxi. 17).   See Bishop Wordsworth's note.

Bards thou shalt have, importunate to sing
  Of gorgeous love, and how the fights were fought;
  Bright songs, with no deep undertone of thought—
Rich jewels sparkling round a meaner thing.

Ah ! how unlike the melody *he* found,
  The shepherd, when his waves of music broke
  Upon the ringing shores of souls, and woke
A two-fold poetry of thought,* and sound !

Thy minstrels shall pass out into the dark,
  The flowers of language change 'neath other skies—
  On alien tongues their delicacy dies—
God only stamps a universal mark.

No son of thine, a flush upon his brow,
  Shall sink with many sunsets to the West ;
  No travell'd breezes give him far-off rest,
No virgin waters sing around his prow.

Lay we such triumph by, 'tis none of thine !
  Thou drinkest not from any peaceful cup ;
  When the wild tribes are out, and standards up,
Of blood—blood red, the colour of thy wine :

  From distant mountains, from the lone hill ledge,
  The Arabs sweep to battle thro' the night,
  Their snowy caftans—a fell line of white—
Showing along the swarthy battle edge ;

As on that impious day when, neck to neck
  In one array 'gainst Israel, were seen
  The sons of Moab, with the Hagarene ;
Gebal was there, Ammon, and Amalek. †

* Alluding to the parallelism of Hebrew poetry.
† Psalm lxxiii. 5-7.

And still the picture darkens, till we see
    Only that wondrous contrast, which the pen
    Of Paul has set before the eyes of men,—
The offspring of the bondmaid, and the free.*

Not thine, O Ishmael, the gain and loss,
    The gloom and gleam of type o'er Isaac's race,
    That brighten'd on to an immortal Face,
And deepen'd to the shadow of the Cross.

For thee no recompense the ages hold,
    No God Incarnate springing from thy line ;
    On earth no Virgin with a Son Divine ;
In heaven no eastern star's prophetic gold.

Oh, " wild, not free," the slave-born's deepest brand !—
    Imprison'd in a changeless mould of mind,
    With passions shifting like the shifting wind,
And hand still lifted 'gainst the lifted hand.

If less the height of grace, then less the fall,
    Less gifted having wander'd less away.
    Thou hast no brightest and no darkest day,
No Bethlehem, no Pilate's judgment-hall.

If, for thy fault, the outcast Hagar trod
    Lone paths of grief, how is it not the worst,
    The drearest fate, and more than twice accurst
To be the Hagar of the Church of God !

Still Isaac wanders over land and sea,
    Stopping betimes with men a little while ;
    There is unfathom'd sadness in his smile,
As one who looks for what has been to be.

* Gal. iv. 22, sqq.

Still, in that thirsty land where it befell
   That one for mortal streams who thirsted sore,
   But needing the immortal waters more,
Found, Hagar-like, her Lord beside the well ;

Oh, still by Sion, and where Jordan runs,
   Over against his waterfalls dark grey
   The Arabs pitch their nomad tents to-day
Upon the land that knoweth not her sons.

But not for ever—it shall yet be well ;
   And when this tyranny is overpast,
   Deep respite from unquiet find at last
Alike God's Isaac and His Ishmael.

Enough of fret and fever—he is gone ;
   Long ages since he yielded up his breath ;
   Why should he live so sadly after death ?
Leave him to sleep, and let the world pass on.

Seek not to raise again the broken psalm,
   So strangely utter'd to the desert sky ;
   After quick throbbing, it is sweet to die,
And take a deep exchange of awful calm.

Freely, as one not having aught to hide,
   Before his brethren's faces to the last,
   Softly and gallantly the wild soul pass'd ;
Homelike and hero-like the death he died.*

So rest in death's dark tent beyond thy wars,
   Where noise of battle doth for ever cease,
   Nor earthly weeping break upon thy peace,
Under the brimm'd eyes of the Eastern stars.

* Gen. xxv. 18.

Q

Dear is the boon that much oblivion gave;
  Not monumental marble for the head,
  But kindly gloom around the quiet dead,—
The requiescat of an unknown grave.

And I, upon the wings of thought would bear
  Thy body from the noise of busy men,
  Into the heart of some untrodden glen,
Far off amid the lustrous mountain air;

There to be buried when the night shall fall,
  In Sinai, a bowshot from the crest,
  Caught like a child, into its mother's breast—
The bosom of the Hagar of St. Paul.*

Robert Jocelyn Alexander.

---

* " For this Agar is Mount Sinai in Arabia." Reiche seems to prove that St. Paul here states (Gal. iv. 24) that locally, in Arabia, Mount Sinai was known by a name equivalent in meaning to Hagar. (" Comment. Crit." *in locum.*)

IV.

SONNETS.

THREE SONNETS SUGGESTED BY SAMUEL RUTHERFORD'S "TRIAL AND TRIUMPH OF FAITH."

I.

Look, if eternally a fair rose grew,
   And if therefrom suns near yet not intense
   Won out a purple-flamèd opulence,
Impassioning the paleness through and through
Eternally beneath the unchanging blue ;
   Then should that rose eternally from thence
   Offer its beauty to the eyes and sense.
And if eternally some mother knew
Her gentle babe in malediction born
   Eternal—but eternally most weak,
Eternal—but eternally forlorn,
   Then should she aye have words of ruth to speak,
And from the mother to her child of woe
For ever should the sweet compassion flow.

II.

The roses and the mothers cannot choose
   But give forth what of beautiful they have,
   But give forth what fair love and sunshine gave
In tender sympathy, or in delicate hues,

Soft scents eternal, love's undying dews.
　　And He who bore the man's heart from earth's wave
　　To Heaven's calm shore that He might sweetly save,
Cannot but pity as our wail renews.
Fragrant eternally were the eternal rose,
　　Eternal were compassion for the child,
　　　Eternal are our sorrows in His sight ;
And everlastingly compassion flows
　　From Him who bears Humanity undefiled,
　　　For the infinite pathos pity infinite.

III.

Prayer is not eloquence nor measured tone
　　Nor memory musical of periods fair.
　　The son forlorn forgetteth half his prayer.*
Faith sighs its prayers, or weeps them with long moan,
With tears that have a grammar of their own.
　　Babes have no words, but only weep or e'er
　　The mother reads the little hunger there.
Faith looks its prayers.　Behold, before the throne
There be full many love-looks of the saints ;
　　And David's upward glance from the earth's snow
　　To God's long spring, three thousand years ago,
Is mark'd in Heaven's best hymn-book of complaints.†
　　Ah! the best prayers that faith may ever think
　　Are untranslatable by pen and ink.

　　　* Luke xv. 18, 19, compared with ver. 21.
　　　† Psalm v. 3.

THE PRINCESS ALICE.

I.

CHILD, with the soft hymn by a father's bed
   Sung soothing ; maiden, whose bright face did stir
   All our rough England with the love of her,
For the dear help she gave the aching head
Of our good Queen—beyond all sung or said
   Of fair adventure and of golden skies
   The morning dawn'd for those delighted eyes ;—
Woman most happy, most serenely wed !
Is there aught better, aught that angels care
   To look on more intensely as they pass
   In their ascension to the sea of glass,
Than lives thus delicate, thus supremely fair :
   In double coronation, double state,
   Twice beautified—twice crown'd by birth and fate ?

II.

Sweet watcher by the wounded,—undefiled
   Pitier, in whom earth's fallen might behold
   The crystal's purity without its cold,—
Pale passionate weeper o'er a princely child,—
Thoughtful and thorough learner of the mild

But difficult lesson Charity can unfold,—
  Calm honest thinker, gently overbold,
Who for a little trod the glacial road
Of doubt, but found it more than doubly sweet
  After the silence of the awful space,
  After the absence of Christ's living face,
To clasp with her cut hands the bleeding feet.
  More beauty than in beauty's self may be
  In thought-won faith and grief, as angels see.

III.

The brightness and the shadow finely blent,
  The beauty and the sorrow, all the twin
  Delight and desolation have pass'd in
Behind the veil; and our Princess present,
Not with the white face of a monument,
  But with a wondrous look of vanish'd sin,
  And such serenity as only win
Souls that have fought their way to full content.
So be she seen by love that ne'er forgets,
  Pathetic with such pathos as God wills—
But a fair influence soothing all regrets,
  A presence on the happy Highland hills,
A memory like the breath of violets
  In letters from a land that sunshine fills.

1879.

TWO SONNETS FROM THE OLD TESTAMENT.

I.

"Hold not Thy peace at my tears."

WHAT is the saddest sweetest lowest sound
   Nearest akin to perfect silence?   Not
   The delicate whisper sometimes in the hot
Autumnal morning heard the cornfields round;
Nor yet to lonely man, now almost bound
   By slumber, near his house a murmuring river
Buzzing and droning o'er the stones for ever.
Not such faint voice of Autumn oat-encrown'd,
And not such liquid murmur, O my heart!
   But tears that drop o'er graves, and sins, and fears,
   A sound the very weeper scarcely hears,
A music in which silence hath some part.
O Thou, all gentle, who all-hearing art,
   Hold not thy peace, sweet Saviour, at my tears.

II.

" And the coast descended unto the river Kanah (brook of reeds),
southwards." (Joshua xvii. 9.)

THE coast descended to the brook of reeds,
    The river Kanah, southward.   In the stream
    The armour of Manasseh used to gleam,
Marching right up to do those daring deeds
Upon the Canaanite.   Wave to wave succeeds,
    O ancient river, age succeeds to age.
    I ask thee nothing of the battle's rage,
Or how the hewing of the forest speeds
In the land of giants.   Only I would know,
    Do those old reeds within thy channel quiver,
Making a music when the breezes blow?
    And do their mottled lances slant as ever?
Do they outlive man's strength—God's weakest things,
Of older race than all our lives of kings?

THE LIGHTED BUILDING.

There is a building by yon river lone
  And walking homewards, upon wintry nights,
  When on the thorn the bitter north wind smites,
And in mine ear the rustling broom makes moan,—
Or on some mild dusk evening, ere hath shone
  The moonlight on the Mourne,—the place doth seem
  A blank and purposeless pile beside the stream.
But suddenly lit up, mine eye hath known
A line of lustrous windows all ablaze ;—
  A palace of enchantment exquisite,
  A fairy fabric self-illuminated :—
Dark building of God's word ! with what amaze
  The heart surveys thee, what time thou art lit
As from within by Him who thee created.

Camus, 1862.

THOUGHTS BY THE SEA.

I.

I HAD been reading Paul's great argument,
  Where, after those strange chapters, darkly penn'd,
  He bursts out with ὦ βάθος at the end ;
When—whether thought or memory might present
Such picture—lo ! a galleon was bent
  Under reef'd topsails through a strait to drop.
  Hung o'er with cliffs that almost touch'd at top.
Dark o'er the dreary sea the vessel went,
Till instantaneously she had pass'd through
  A touch of moonlight on her sails ; before her,
  World without end, the waves ; the blue sky o'er her.
Behold, I thought, an image grandly true !
  After Predestination's narrow road
  The silver ocean of the Love of God.

II.

A hot day in September.   A white mist
  Clung to the vale, and up the hill a blur,
  As of thin smoke, part blue, part silverer,
Stretch'd o'er the corn.   The ripples lazily kiss'd
As on the bent I lay their sound to list.

Between Lough Swilly and the mountain spur
I saw a green down stretch without a stir.
A curlew was the only harmonist.
The sole shapes there were gulls, that in the heat
   Strutted upon the sward a space and back,
   White-plumed; and crows, like crones in shawls of black
Dropp'd glossy from the shoulders to the feet.
   But far afield, howe'er the day may burn,
   Harvesters work—and that is much to learn.

"*A WINTER GALE IN THE CHANNEL.*"

(PAINTED BY HENRY MOORE.)

I.

I LOVE this ocean picture's pale reserve :
  No tints unnatural of purpling grain,
    Azure, or opal, mar the rough grey main,
The sweep, the swing, the long froth-churning curve,
The shore-ward working and confusèd swerve
    Of yellowing water —white blooms wear such stain,
    All dashed and muddied with the April rain.
No poor ambition did the painter nerve !
Well that no laboured ship or sun-burst broke
    The strong monotony of that sky and surge.
Leave, only leave, the line of stormy smoke,
    The sea-birds dashed upon the nearer verge,—
Brave in its truth this ocean piece shall be
The type for us of Homer's harvestless sea.

II.

Nor only this—lesson of more than art !
  Who dares, strong in simplicity, despise
  The evanescent beauties that arise
Before his gaze, and, in true thought apart,

Look on straight forward to life's very heart :
  Who dares, by gift supernal rendered wise,
  Deem truth more beautiful for all true eyes
Than garish things made merely for the mart ;
Whether he paint or write or live his thought,
  To that which he produces shall be lent
  An immortality of ravishment,
One day it shall be own'd divinely wrought ;
  And all the sternness of its strength shall be
  Like the grave beauty of this pictured sea.

FIVE SONNETS.

I.

WHAT love I when I love Thee, O my God?
  Not corporal beauty, nor the limb of snow,
  Nor of loved light the white and pleasant flow,
Nor manna showers, nor streams that flow abroad,
Nor flowers of Heaven, nor small stars of the sod:
  Not these, my God, I love, who love Thee so;
  Yet love I something better than I know:—
A certain light on a more golden road;
A sweetness, not of honey or the hive;
  A beauty, not of summer or the spring;
  A scent, a music, and a blossoming
Eternal, timeless, placeless, without gyve,
  Fair, fadeless, undiminish'd, ever dim,—
  This, this is what I love in loving Him.

II.

This, this is what I love, and what is this?
  I ask'd the beautiful earth, who said—"not I."
  I ask'd the depths, and the immaculate sky
And all the spaces said—"not He but His."
And so, like one who scales a precipice,

Height after height, I scaled the flaming ball
    Of the great universe, yea, pass'd o'er all
The world of thought, which so much higher is.
Then I exclaimed. "To whom is mute all murmur
    Of phantasy, of nature, and of art,
He, than articulate language hears a firmer
    And grander meaning in his own deep heart.
No sound from cloud or angel." Oh, to win
That voiceless voice—" My servant, enter in "!

III.

MEMORY.

IDEAS FADING IN THE MEMORY.

QUICKLY they vanish to a land unlit,
    Things for which no man cares to smile or mourn,
    Forgotten in the place where they were born;
Each hath a marvellous history unwrit,
A fathomless river floweth over it.
    Quickly they fade, with no more traces worn
    Than shadows flying over fields of corn
Wear, as in soft processional they flit.
The thought (much like the children of our youth)
    Doth often die before us, and presents
    The very semblance of the monuments
To which we are approaching aye in sooth,
    Where, though the brass and marble do not waste,
    The tints are faded, and the line effaced.*

---

* See Locke, " On the Human Understanding," book ii., chap. x.,
§§ 4, 5.

IV.

REVIVAL OF MEMORY.

Sadly, O sage, thine images are told.
　Think we of cornfields, where again there fall,
　At Memory's touch that is so magical,
All the long lights that ever rippled gold
Across their surface, all the manifold
　Wavelets of tremulous shadow; and withal
　Through doors and windows of a haunted hall, .
Those buried children of the days of old,
Those evanescent children of dead years,
　Clouded or glorious, glide into the room,
　Sudden as yellow leaves drop from the tree;
And all the moulder'd imagery reappears,
　And all the letter'd lines are fair to see,
　And all the legend lives above the tomb.

V.

MARVELS OF MEMORY.

Strange dying, resurrection stranger yet!
　In the deep chamber, Memory, let me dwell,
　Folded in a recess ineffable.
Lo! in that silent chamber sometimes set,
I music hear, and breath of violet
　(Though flowers be none within a mile to smell)
　From breath of lily I can finely tell,
And I with joy remember my regret,
　And I, regretful, think how glad I was.
O men who roam to see world-famous tracts,
　Immaculate skies, or from the mountain-pass
The great white wonder of the cataracts,
　Visits to many a lovely land ye weave
　In looms of fancy—but *yourselves* ye leave.*

* St. Augustine, "Confess.," lib. x., 12, 13, 14.

ST. JOHN AT PATMOS.

I.

WHAT be his dreams in Patmos?   O'er the seas
   Looks he toward Athens, where the very fall
   Of Grecian sunlight is Platonical?
Or, peradventure, towards the Cyclades,
The Delian earth-star, ray'd with laurel-trees—
   From ribbon'd baskets where Demeter threw
   Flowers the colour of the country blue
Oat-garlanded in Paros—or where bees
Humming o'er Amalthæa, who fed Zeus
   With goat-milk, goldenly the forest starr'd
While rosy purple apples, full of juice,
   Laugh'd in the grassy horn—where, Naxosward,
Flush'd Dyonysus, driven o'er the brine,
Ivied the mast, and cream'd the crimson wine.

II.

Not fancies of the soft Ionian clime,
   Nor thoughts on Plato's page, that greener grow
   Than do the plane-trees by the pleasant flow
Of the Ilissus in the summer time,
Came to the Galilean with sweet chime.

Blanch'd in the blaze of Syrian summers lo !
He gazes on Gennesareth, aglow
Within its golden mountain cup sublime.
The sunset comes. Behind the Roman tower
    The dark boat's circled topsails shift and swell,
The tunick'd boatmen dip their nets an hour,
    And the sun goeth down on Jezreel.
Quench'd is the flickering furnace of the dust,
The mountains branded as with red gold dust.

III.

But ere heaven's cressets burn along its plain,
    The Master comes.   And as a man, all night
    Lull'd in a room full fronting ocean's might,
First waking sees a whiteness on his pane,
A little dawning whiteness, then again
    A little line insufferably bright
    Edging the ripples, orbing on outright
Until the glory he may scarce sustain ;
And as a mighty city far-off kenn'd,
    Although the same, from each new height and glen
    Looks strangely different to the merchantmen
Who in long files towards its ramparts wend ; —
    So to St. John's deep meditative eye,
    That Nature grew to God's own majesty.

THE LAST DAY OF SUMMER.

ALL the sweet summer azure is not fled—
    What hath the woodland, then, to do with grief?
    The apparition of a yellow leaf,
The half-suspected russet overhead—
Of this it dreams, and is disquieted.
    Snowdrops and other dainty things as brief,
    Whereof the young anemones were chief,
The tremulous anemones are dead.
    Long since the snowdrops have been fain to die ;
    Long since the anemones have pass'd away :
Some colour'd leaves discolour every morn—
    Touch'd by the thought of which chronology
The trees have something that they long to say,
Inaudible, multitudinous, forlorn.

August 31, 1885.

V.

TRANSLATIONS.

VIRGILII ÆNEIS. LIB. VI. 1–281.

ANGLICÉ REDDITA.

I.

So he speaks weeping, and speeds on full sail
  To Cumæ, the Eubœan city hoar.
Oceanward, safe at last from surf and gale,
  The sailors turn their prows. Their perils o'er,
  The anchor stays them, and they rock no more.
Far, far along with ships the strand is lined ;
  The merry men leap on the Hesperian shore ;
Part strike the seeds of flame from flints, part wind
Swift through the leafy lairs, and forest fountains find.

II.

But good Æneas seeks the shrine exalted
  Where, in his glory on the mountain height,
Apollo rules — and the weird cave o'ervaulted
  With the far secrecy of awful night,
  The Sybil's home. Her mighty mind and sprite
The Delian seer doth evermore inspire,
  And touch the opening future with his light.
They enter Trivia's grove, and much admire
The temple's dazzling lines, fretted with golden fire.

III.

They say self-exiled Dædalus, going forth
   From Minos' realms with pinions swift and bold,
Dared trust him to the sky, and swam far north
   Way unattempted ! to the Arcti cold.
    Lightly, at last, o'er Cumæ's ancient hold
Self-poised he hung, and first from air set free,
   Treading this firm green earth, his vow enroll'd,
To dedicate the wings that oar'd the sea
Of the blue sky, in fanes, O Phœbus, built for thee !

IV.

The fane is built.   Lo ! the doors sculptured here
   Androgeos' death.   This side the Athenians stand,
Ah me ! in act to yield their seven a year.
   The urn is there ; the lot is in the hand.
   Opposite answers the fair Gnossian land,
Ridg'd o'er the ocean with its rise and fall.
   Behold ! the beautiful bull, the evil-plann'd
Adultery of Pasiphaë, and withal
The twy-form'd child, the pledge of love unnatural.

V.

Here, too, stands sculptured the much-labour'd place,
   The inextricable labyrinth, and how the untold
Love pangs of that poor Queen did bring her grace
   From Dædalus.   Within his hands behold,
   Guiding blind steps, the thread that might unfold
The maze.   O Icarus ! thou wouldst prevail
   In that fair piece to win large space of gold ;
But sorrow marr'd his art—to carve the tale
A father's hands twice o'er were raised, twice o'er to fail.

VI.

All this had they perused with eager eyne,
  Had not Achates come, and by his side,
Priestess and prophetess of birth divine,
  Deiphobe.   " Not this the time or tide,
  O King!" she said, "on metal glorified
By sculpture to stand eye-charm'd.   Rather crave
  The hour and the god, seven steers by yoke untried,
Seven ewes of ritual meetness."   These they have
Full soon, and follow her down to her mountain cave.

VII.

An antre in a scaur of the old world—
  A hundred subterranean avenues broad
Lead to its hundred mouths, whence back is hurl'd
  The Sibyl's hundred-echoed voice.   They trod
  The threshold, when, " The god!" behold the god!
" 'Tis time to interrogate the Fates," she said;
  And saying, neither face nor hair abode
In natural wise—apant she was with dread,
And all her long hair stood abristle on her head.

VIII.

Greater she look'd and taller ;—superhuman
  The majesty and the music of her tone ;—
The inspiration of a mortal woman
  Breath'd by a deity now nearer grown.
  "Cease not," she cries, "thy prayers, thy vows make
    known.
Not without this of darkness shall yon gate
  Astonish'd ope, for things inanimate own
The power of prayer."—She ceased, chill fear thereat
Curdled the Teucris frame : with accents passionate,

IX.

From his deep heart their King made supplication :
  "O Phœbus ! pitiful of Troy's unrest,
Who gav'st the Dardan shaft its inclination
    From the hand of Paris to the heroic breast
    Of great Æacides !   Lands the loneliest
In old mysterious Afric, thee for guide,
    With fields long stretch'd by sand-banks low of crest
Has my bark touch'd, and regions wild and wide,
Silverly ring'd around by the untravell'd tide.

X.

" And now at last our breath is on the brow
    Of Italy ; we grasp the fair form flying
O'er the blue sea illusive.   Until now
    Troy's fortune follows us.   Your heavy lying
    Vengeance from Illium, no more defying
Your godhead, by her glory, adverse powers !
    Remove.   And thou, with voice prophetic, crying,
Let rest my people (lo ! we ask but ours),
And my disquieted gods at last in Latium's bowers.

XI.

" So, twins Latonian ! shall a marble shrine
    Of massy proof to ye be dedicate.
So shall dawn days of song and sun and wine,
    Days of high festival in my future state—
    Call'd by the náme of Phœbus.   There await
Thee, too, O Sibyl ! places deep and dread,
    And chosen men to keep thy words of fate.
Only these awful lines of thine be said,
Not written on light leaves by wild winds scatterèd."

XII.

But like the steed untaught to bear its master
  Plunges the seer, if so be she may skill
To fling the Presence from her.   He, the faster,
  On the foam'd mouth and fierce heart pressing still,
  Wearies her out, and curbs her at his will.
The hundred entrances open suddenly,
  And on the breezes doth this answer thrill :
"The land hath wilder storms than sweep the sea;
Safe from the perilous deep these storms are waiting thee."

XIII.

Ah ! to Lavinium (this thou need'st not dread)
  The sons of Dædalus shall come, full fain
That they had come not.   Battles, and battle-red
  With foam discolour'd, I behold amain
  The Tiber rolling.   On that fatal plain
Camps shall not want ; nor yet another river
  New Simois or Xanthus ; nor again
A new and goddess-born Achilles,—never
Shall Juno cease to haunt thy hated race for ever.

XIV.

"Then in those days, calamitous indeed,
  Alliances thy pride shall stoop to sue ;
The cause of so much woe again decreed
  A foreign bride, unto the Trojans true.
  But thou, what ills soever may come anew,
Bate not a jot of heart or hope—nor cease
  To go right forward, as the boldest do,
Far as their fortune.   The first way of peace,
Little as thou may'st deem, comes from the side of Greece."

XV.

With such-like sentences the Sibyl sings
    Dree in her voiceful cave, and darkly weaves
Her words obscure round truly boded things.
    Such rein, such goad hath Phœbus.   But when leaves
    The inspiration the wild heart it heaves,
And the pale lips, quieted, foam no more,
    Begins Æneas—" Nought here freshly grieves,
No new face unexpected rises o'er
The sea of woe ; my heart has traversed it before.

XVI.

" One only boon, since here is the hell-portal,
    The shadowy marish, Acheron's overflow ;
Ah ! let me see my dear Sire's face immortal,
    And teach thou me the way that I must go.
    Him from the city flaming far below
I bare upon these shoulders, shaft and dart
    Raining by thousands after.   Winds that blow
Angrily o'er the seas we sail'd athwart.
Heaven that he braved with me, was this an old man's heart ?

XVII.

" By his command I come with supplication ;
    Pity a son and father !   Lo, 'twere meet ;
For not in vain hath Hecate thy station
    Fixed o'er the under-world.   By those most sweet
    Harp-strings of his, if Orpheus won to greet
His consort's ghost ; if Pollux walketh well,
    For brother-love, with oft-returning feet
Death's awful road ; what boots me now to tell
Theseus, Alcides, and my birth of miracle ? "

XVIII.

He said, and grasp'd the altar.   She spake then :
  " Not to descend (descent most easy is !),
Child of the blood of Gods and godlike men !
  Not to descend (for ever more dark Dis
  Keeps his gates open)—up from the abyss
Earthward to walk, and feel the upper breeze,
  This is the work of works, the labour this.
None have attain'd it, save few souls who please
High Jove, by virtue borne to starry palaces.

XIX.

" All the vast interspace is night-black forest,
  Embay'd by dark Cocytus round and round.
If then that toil, the emptiest yet sorest,
  So please thy spirit, twice to wander bound
  Across the Styx, twice see the shadowy ground,—
Hear what thou hast to do.   A bough all golden
  Lieth perdu in a thick tree.   The encrown'd
Hell-empress claims it.   All the forest's olden
Immeasurable depths about the bough are folden.

XX.

" But none without the gathering of the tree's
  Growth that hath golden leafage ever may
Enter that obscure country.   So decrees
  She who demands the gift—Proserpina.
  Ever as one such bough is rent away
Leafs me another of the self-same stuff.
  Look well : pluck quickly.   Eathes it follows aye
Whom the fates favour.   Otherwise, no rough
Effort can conquer it ; no steel is sharp enough.

XXI.

Now, whilst thou lingerest here inquiring much,
   A friend's corpse lies unburied by the foam
Unknown to thee; and death's defiling touch
    The fleet contaminates.   First it doth become
    To bear the dead man to his own long home ;
Bring dark-fleeced victims, expiate the dead,
   So through the Stygian realm thy feet may roam.'
Long silence kept she when these words were said :
Æneas left the cave, downcast, in drearihead.

XXII.

Much he resolves these issues, dark and blind ;
   Much with his dear Achates, faithful mate
Who walks beside, with equal cares of mind,
    Surmises, what companion deadly fate
    May have incurr'd—who lies in such estate.
Behold ! they see Misenus on the strand
   By deed unworthy done to death of late.
None better breath'd the brass—that master hand
Brave hearts has often thrill'd, and flames of battle fann'd.

XXIII.

Once with his spear and clarion, in glory,
   He used to walk the thickest of the fight,
Great Hector's comrade.   But when Hector gory
    Lay by Achilles slain, the heroic wight
    Follow'd Æneas, no inferior light.
Now while he challenges the gods full stern,
   With bugle blowing o'er the sea forth right,
Him, as they tell, did Triton overturn
Where through the circling rocks the waves for ever churn.

XXIV.

All mourn, Æneas chief.   Tears on each face,
   They do what Sibyl bids.   As altars look
So looks the pyre.   They range an antique chase.
   Fall the funereal pines ; with many a stroke
   The ilex sounds, wedge-cloven is the oak,
Down from the hills the mountain ash they rend.
   Æneas girt him for the work, and spoke
Sadly his thoughts, revolving as he kenn'd
The immeasurable world of wood without an end.

XXV.

" Ah ! if the golden bough upon that tree
   By tell-tale glinting were made visible
Through the great forest !   All too well of thee,
   Misenus, did the seer her bodement spell ;
   Good should there come, too, from the oracle."
Scarce said, when lo ! from heaven, with sweet accord,
   Twin doves flew down (full easy could he tell
His mother's birds), and flash'd on his regard,
And lightly settled down upon the grass-green sward.

XXVI.

Joyful he prays—" Fly gently, doves most fair !
   An' there be way, oh gently fly and guide
Your happy course directing through the air
   To the rich turf that ever doth abide,
   By opulent shadows strangely glorified
Under the Bough miraculous.   Mother mine,
   Goddess and mother, at this doubtful tide
Fail not thy son."   He halted with strain'd eyne,
Watching what course they took, expectant of a sign.

S

XXVII.

Graceful they glided on with many a pause,
　Now fluttering, now feeding,—never lost
Quite from his ken, till o'er Avernus' jaws,
　Whose pitchy breath by light wings is uncross'd,
　Lapsing through liquid air upon that most
Desirèd seat, the enchanted tree, they sit.
　There, through the duller boughs, one gold-emboss'd,
With a reverberated glimmer lit,
Twinkled atween the leaves, discolour exquisite.

XXVIII.

Like as, in winter cold, in sylvan places,
　No produce of its tree, comes a strange green,
And round great stems, like pillars, interlaces
　Its delicate network's crocus-colour'd sheen,—
　Like as the mistletoe in wood is seen,
Such on the shadowy ilex-tree withal,
　Look'd the gold growing its dark leaves between ;
So came there to the low wind's rise and fall
Metallic tinkling, thin, and faintly musical.

XXIX.

It, seeming loth to part, incontinent
　Æneas plucks, and to the Sibyl brings.
But on the shore the Teucri made lament,
　And to the ashes bare their offerings
　That have no gratitude for mortal things.
A pyre funereal high aloft they raise,
　All rich and resinous for the fire's strong wings.
Dark leaves enweave it.　Trophies of his frays,
On cypresses of bale they hang his arms ablaze.

XXX.

Part haste the boiling cauldron all a-bubble,
    Wash the cold corpse, anoint it, and make moan.
Then on the bed that never shall know trouble
    They place the limbs, and over them are thrown
    The purple vestments that are so well known.
Part stoop below the bier (a woeful toil),
    Holding the torch averse, as erst was done.
Fiercely and yet more fierce do the flames boil,
With frankincense flung in and flesh and cups of oil.

XXXI.

After the fallen flame had ceas'd to burn,
    They pour'd wine on the ashes all athirst ;
And Corynæus in a brazen urn
    Gather'd the bones, his comrades thrice aspersed
    With dew from happy olive, ere he durst
Breathe the last words.　Æneas on a hoar
    Headland the arms wherein the man was versed,
Hung high above his sepulchre, trump and oar.
The trumpeter's name that cliff beareth for evermore.

XXXII.

This done, he executes the seer's behest.
    There was a grotto, pebble-strewn and vast :
Safe was it folden by the inkiest
    Of lakes, and shadows falling thick and vast
    From the great woods.　Above it never pass'd
Bright bird unstricken—such a reek there goes
    From its jaws ever to the sky o'ercast.
Four dark-back'd steers the maid doth now dispose,
And pours the sacred wine slope down between their
    brows.

XXXIII.

Taking atop the bristly tufts betwixt
  Their horns, she gives the fire the first libation,
Invoking Hecate, whose sway is fix'd
  In heav'n and hell.   The others in their station
  Bring knives.   The spirting blood for expiation
They catch in bowls.   Æneas smites amain
  A dark-fleeced lamb, the due propitiation
To the great daughters of old Chaos twain.
A barren heifer, too, for Hecate is slain.

XXXIV.

Thus does he auspicate to the Stygian sire
  His altar of the night, and minister
For the steer's entrails heap'd upon the fire
  The outpour'd oil.   Lo! many a mountain spur
  With all its woods is wondrously astir,
Soon as the dawn begins to streak the dark;
  And as the goddess-presence nears, for her
Bellows the earth, and through the shadows, hark!
Deep-baying all the hounds of hell begin to bark.

XXXV.

" Far hence," the prophetess exclaims, "far hence
  Be ye who are profane from all the land!
Much need, Æneas, of the heroic sense
  And the firm soul.   March onward, sword in hand!"
  She said, and plunged into the cave, and grand,
With fearless steps, he follow'd her right on.
  Gods of the manes! voiceless shadows! wann'd
And silent places lighted of no sun,
Oh, suffer me to speak, Chaos and Phlegethon!

XXXVI.

Darkling they walk'd beneath the lonely night,
  On through the shadows, through the tenantless homes,
Realms unsubstantial.   Look ! such dubious light,
  Malign and chequer'd, to the traveller comes,
  Belated far aforest, when there glooms,
Rather than shines, a moon in clouded skies
  Upon a colourless world.   Before the rooms,
Hell's antechambers couchant, there he eyes
Sorrow's and conscience's avenging mysteries.

XXXVII.

Yon is the home of Sickness, pale and pining,
  Old age, and Fear, and Famine, that can win
To evil deed,—of Poverty entwining
  Misery with Shame,—of Death, and Labour's din,
  And Sleep, Death's brother and his next of kin.
Over against them, and against the lair
  Of those ill joys that are the foulest sin,
War on the threshold stands,—and Discord there,
With ribbons blood-bedropp'd woven through her snaky
     hair.

THE EMPEROR'S RETURN.*

TRANSLATED FROM VICTOR HUGO.

"Il disait, 'Oh je reviendrai.'"

SIRE! to thy capital thou shalt come back,
  Without the battle's tocsin and wild stir;
Beneath the arch, drawn by eight steeds coal black,
    Dress'd like an Emperor.

Thro' this same portal, God accompanying,
  Sire! thou shalt come upon the car of state;
Like Charlemagne, a high ensainted King,
    Like Cæsar, wondrous great.

On thy gold sceptre, to be vanquish'd never,
  Thy crimson beakèd bird shall shine anon.
Upon thy mantle all thy bees ashiver
    Shall twinkle in the sun.

Paris shall light up all her high and hundred
  Tow'rs, shall speak out with all her tones sublime;
Bells, clarions, rolling drums shall all be thunder'd
    In music at a time.

* These translations from Victor Hugo were executed jointly by my
wife and myself.

A mighty people, pale, with steps that falter,
  Shall come to thee, by one attraction drawn,
Awe-stricken as a Priest before the altar,
    Glad as a child at dawn,—

A people who would lay all laws e'er sung
  Or storied at thy feet—aye floating on,
Intoxicate, from Bonaparte the young
    To old Napoleon.

Then a new army, burning for the advance,
  In exploit terrible, round thy car shall cry
Amain, " Vive l'Empereur!" and " Vive la France!"
    And seeing thee pass by,

Chief of the mighty Empire! down shall fall
  People and troops—but thou before their view
Shalt not be able to stoop down at all
    With—" I am pleased with you."

An acclamation, tender, lofty, sweet,
  A heart-song high as ecstasy can bear it,
Shall fill, O Captain mine! the city's street,
    But thou shalt never hear it.

Stern Grenadiers, the veterans we admire,
  Mute thy steed's steps shall kiss—albeit
A sight pathetic, beautiful, yet, sire!
    Your majesty shall not see it.

While round thy form gigantic, like a friend,
  France and the world awake in shadows deep,
Here in thy Paris ever, world without end,
    Thou shalt lie fast asleep—

Ay, fast asleep with that same sullen slumber,
   Those fadeless dreams that on his stone chair fix
The Barbarossa, sitting out that number
    Of centuries now six.

Thy sword beside thee, and thine eyelids close,
   Thy hand yet moved by Bertrand's kiss—the last,—
Upon the bed whence sleeper never rose,
    Thou shalt be stretch'd full fast.

Like to those soldiers marching bolt upright,
   So often after thee to field or town,
Who by the wind of battle touch'd one night
    Suddenly laid them down

Like sleepers, not like those whose race is run,
   With grave proud attitude of armèd men—
But them that voice of dawn, the morning gun,
    Shall never wake again.

Yea, so much like, that seeing thee all ice,
   Like a mute god permitting adoration,
They who came smiling love-drunk, in a trice,
    Shall raise a lamentation.

Sire ! at that moment thou, for kingdom meet,
   Shalt have all beating hearts to be thine own.
Nations shall make thy phantom take a seat,
    A universal throne.

Poets select, upon their knees in dust,
   Shall hail thee far diviner than of old,
And gild thine altar, stain'd by hands unjust,
    With a sublimer gold.

The clouds shall pass away from thy great glory;
   Nothing to trouble it for aye shall come.
It shall expand itself o'er all our story,
     Like a vast azure dome.

Yea, thou shalt be to all a presence solemn,
   Both good and great,—to France an exile high
And calm—a brass Colossus on thy column
     To every stranger's eye.

But thou, the while the sacred pomp shall lead
   A cortege such as time hath never heard,
So that all eyes shall seem to see indeed
     A vanish'd world upstirr'd;

The while they hear (hard by the wondrous dome
   Where shadows keep the great names that men mark
In Paris still) the old guns growling home
     Their master with a bark;

The while thy name without a peer shall soar,
   Illustrious, beautiful, to Heav'n,—ah ! thou
Shalt in the darkness feel for evermore
     The grave-worm on thy brow.

BOAZ ASLEEP.

TRANSLATED FROM VICTOR HUGO.

AT work within his barn since very early,
   Fairly tired out with toiling all the day,
   Upon the small bed where he always lay
Boaz was sleeping by his sacks of barley.

Barley and wheat-fields he possess'd, and well,
   Though rich, loved justice; wherefore all the flood
   That turn'd his mill-wheels was unstain'd with mud,
And in his smithy blazed no fire of hell.

His beard was silver, as in April all
   A stream may be.   He did not grudge a stook:
   When the poor gleaner pass'd, with kindly look,
Quoth he, " Of purpose let some handfuls fall."

He walk'd his way of life straight on, and plain,
   With justice cloth'd, like linen white and clean;
   And ever rustling toward the poor, I ween,
Like public fountains ran his sacks of grain.

Good master, faithful friend, in his estate
   Frugal, yet generous beyond the youth,
   He won regard of woman; for, in sooth,
The young man may be fair, the old man's great.

Life's primal source, unchangeable and bright,
   The old man entereth, the day eterne;
   For in the young man's eye a flame may burn,
But in the old man's eye one seeth light.

As Jacob slept, or Judith, so full deep
   Slept Boaz 'neath the leaves. Now it betided,
   Heaven's gate being partly open, that there glided
A fair dream forth, and hover'd o'er his sleep.

And in his dream, to heav'n, the blue and broad,
   Right from his loins an oak-tree grew amain;
   His race ran up it far in a long chain.
Below it sang a king, above it died a God.

Whereupon Boaz murmured in his heart,
   " The number of my years is past fourscore
   How may this be? I have not any more,
Or son, or wife; yea, she who had her part

" In this my couch, O Lord! is now in thine.
   And she half living, I half dead within,
   Our beings still commingle, and are twin.
It cannot be that I should found a line.

" Youth hath triumphal mornings ; its days bound
   From night as from a victory. But such
   A trembling as the birch-trees to the touch
Of winter is on eld, and evening closes round.

" I bow my soul to death, as kine to meet
   The water bow their fronts athirst," he said.
   The cedar feeleth not the rose's head,
Nor he the woman's presence at his feet.

For while he slept, the Moabitess Ruth
  Lay at his feet expectant of his waking.
  He knowing not what sweet guile she was making;
She knowing not what God would have in sooth.

Asphodel scents did Gilgal's breezes bring—
  Through nuptial shadows, questionless, full fast
  The angels sped, for momently there pass'd
A something blue which seemed to be a wing.

Silent was all in Jezreel and Ur;
  The stars were glittering in the heav'ns dusk meadows,
  Far west, among those flow'rs of the shadows,
The thin clear crescent, lustrous over her,

Made Ruth raise question, looking through the bars
  Of heaven with eyes half-oped, what god, what comer
  Unto the harvest of the eternal summer,
Had flung his golden hook down on the field of stars.

THE ROSE OF THE INFANTA.

TRANSLATED FROM VICTOR HUGO.

SHE is so little—in her hand a rose ;
A stern duenna watches where she goes.
What sees she?   Ah, she knows not—the clear shine
Of waters shadow'd by the birch and pine.
What lies before?—a swan with silver wing,
The wave that murmurs to the branch's swing,
Or the deep garden flourishing below?
Fair as an angel frozen into snow,
The royal child looks on, and hardly seems to know.

As in a depth of glory far away,
Down the green park, a lofty palace lay.
There drank the deer from many a crystal pond,
And the starr'd peacock gemm'd the shade beyond.
Around that child all nature seem'd more bright,
Her innocence was as an added light.
Rubies and diamonds strew'd the path she trode,
And jets of sapphire from the dolphins flow'd.
Still at the water's side she holds her place.
Her bodice bright is set with Genoa lace.

O'er her rich robe, through every satin fold,
Wanders an arabesque in threads of gold.
From its green urn the rose, unfolding grand,
Weighs down the exquisite smallness of her hand.
And when the child bends to the red leaf's tip
Her laughing nostril, and her carmine lip,
The royal flower purpureal kissing there
Hides more than half that young face, bright and fair,
So that the eye, deceived, can scarcely speak
Where shows the rose, or where the rose-red cheek.
Her eyes look bluer from their dark brown frame;
Sweet eyes, sweet form, and Mary's sweeter name.
All joy, enchantment, perfume, waits she there,
Heaven in her glance, her very name a prayer.

Yet 'neath thy sky, and before life and fate,
Poor child, she feels herself so vaguely great.
With stately grace she gives her presence high
To dawn, to spring, to shadows flitting by,
To the dark sunset glories of the heaven,
And all the wild magnificence of even :
On nature waits, eternal and serene,
With all the graveness of a little queen.
She never sees a man but on her knee ;
She Duchess of Brabant one day will be,
And rule Sardinia, or the Flemish crowd—
She is the Infanta, five years old, and proud.

Thus it is with king's children, for they wear
A shadowy circlet on their foreheads fair ;
Their tottering steps are toward a kingly chair.
Calmly she waits, and breathes her gather'd flower
Till one shall cull for her imperial power.
Already her eye saith, " It is my right ; "
Even love flows from her mingled with affright.

If some one, seeing her so fragile stand,
Were it to save her should put forth his hand,
Ere he had made a step, or breath'd a vow,
The scaffold's shadow were upon his brow.

While the child laughs, beyond the bastion thick
Of that vast palace, Roman Catholic,
Whose every turret like a mitre shows,
Behind the lattice something fearful goes.
Men shake to see a shadow from beneath,
Passing from pane to pane, like vapoury wreath,
Pale, black, and still, it glides from room to room,
Or stands a whole day, motionless in its gloom,
In the same spot, like ghost upon a tomb,
Or glues its dark brow to the casement wan,
Dim shade that lengthens as the night draws on.
Its step funereal lingers like the swing
Of passing bell—'tis death, or else the king.

'Tis he, the man by whom men live or die ;
But could one look beyond that phantom eye,
As by the wall he leans a little space,
And see what shadows fill his soul's dark place,
Not the fair child, the waters clear, the flowers
Golden with sunset—not the birds, the bowers—
No ; 'neath that eye, those fatal brows that keep
The fathomless brain, like ocean dark and deep,
There, as in moving mirage, should one find
A fleet of ships that go before the wind :
On the foam'd wave, and 'neath the starlight pale,
The strain and rattle of a fleet in sail,
And through the fog an isle on her white rock,
Hearkening from far the thunder's coming shock.

Still by the water's edge doth silent stand
The Infanta, with the rosebud in her hand,
Caresses it with eyes as blue as heaven.
Sudden a breeze—such breeze as panting even,
From her full heart, flings out to field and brake—
Ruffles the waters, bids the rushes shake,
And makes through all their green recesses swell
The massive myrtle and the asphodel.
To the fair child it comes, and tears away
On its strong wind the rose-flower from the spray,
On the wild waters casts it, bruised and torn,
And the Infanta only holds a thorn.
Frighten'd, perplex'd, she follows with her eyes
Into the basin where her ruin lies,
Looks up to heaven, and questions of the breeze
That had not fear'd her Highness to displease.
But all the pond is changed—anon so clear,
Now black it swells as though with rage and fear;
A mimic sea, its small waves rise and fall,
And the poor rose is broken by them all ;
Its hundred leaves, toss'd wildly round and round,
Beneath a thousand waves are whelm'd and drown'd.
It was a foundering fleet, you might have said.
Quoth the duenna, with her face of shade :
" Madam "—for she had mark'd her ruffled mind—
" All things belong to princes—but the wind."

THE REGIMENT OF BARON MADRUCE.

When the regiment of the halberdiers is proudly marching
    by,
The eagle of the mountain screams from out his stormy sky ;
Who speaketh to the precipice, and to the chasm sheer,
Who hovers o'er the thrones of kings, and bids the caitiffs
    fear.
King of the peak and glaciers, king of the cold white scalps,
He lifts his head, at that close tread, the eagle of the Alps.
Oh, shame ! those men that march below ! oh, ignominy
    dire !
Are the sons of my free mountains, sold for Imperial hire ?
Ah! the vilest of the dungeon, ah ! the slave upon the seas
Is great, is pure, is glorious, is grand compared with these,
Who, born amid my holy rocks in solemn places high,
Where the tall pines bend like rushes when the storm goes
    sweeping by,
Yet give the strength of foot they learn'd by perilous path
    and flood,
And from their blue-eyed mothers won the old mysterious
    blood,

T

'The daring that the good south wind into their nostrils blew,
And the proud swelling of the heart with each pure breath
    they drew ;
The graces of the mountain glens with flowers in summer
    gay,
And all the glory of the hills—to earn a lackey's pay.'
'Their country free and joyous—she of the rugged sides—
She of the rough peaks arrogant, whereon the tempest rides ;
Mother of the unconquer'd thought, and of the savage form ;
Who brings out of her sturdy heart the hero and the storm ;
Who giveth freedom unto man, and life unto the beast ;
Who hears her silver torrents ring, like joy-bells at a feast ;
Who hath her caves for palaces, and, where her chalets stand,
The proud old archer of Altorf, his good bow in his hand ;—
Is she to suckle jailers ?   Shall shame and glory rest
Amid her lakes and mountains, like twins upon her breast ?
Shall the two-headed eagle, mark'd with her double blow,
Drink of her milk through all these hearts whose blood he
    bids to flow ?

*   *   *   *   *

Say, was it pomp ye needed, and all the proud array
Of courtliness and high parade upon a gala day ?
Look up ; have not my valleys their torrents white with
    foam,
Their lines of silver bullion on the green hills of home ?
Doth not sweet May embroider my rocks with pearls and
    flow'rs,
Her fingers trace a richer lace than yours in all my bow'rs ?
Are not my old peaks gilded when the sun rises proud,
And each one shakes a white mist plume out of the thunder-
    cloud ?
O neighbours of the golden sky, sons of the mountain sod,
Why wear a base king's colours for the livery of God ?

Oh, shame ! despair ! to see my Alps their giant shadows
    fling
Into the very waiting-room of tyrant and of king !
O thou deep heaven, unsullied yet, into thy gulfs sublime,
Up azure tracts of flaming light, let my free spirit climb,
Till from my sight, in that clear light, earth and her crimes
    be gone,
The men who act the evil deeds, the caitiffs who look on,
Far far, into that space immense, beyond the vast white veil,
Where distant stars come out and shine, and the great sun
    grows pale.

THE POOR.

TRANSLATED FROM VICTOR HUGO.

'TIS night—within the close-shut cabin door,
  The room is wrapt in shade, save where there fall
Some twilight rays, that creep along the floor,
  And show the fisher's nets upon the wall.

In the dim corner, from the oaken chest
  A few white dishes glimmer; through the shade
Stands a tall bed with dusky curtains drest,
  And a rough mattress at its side is laid.

Five children on the long low mattress lie—
  A nest of little souls, it heaves with dreams;
In the high chimney the last embers die,
  And redden the dark roof with crimson gleams.

The mother kneels and thinks, and, pale with fear,
  She prays alone, hearing the billows shout;
While to wild winds, to rocks, to midnight drear,
  The ominous old ocean sobs without.

Poor wives of fishers! Ah, 'tis sad to say,
  Our sons, our husbands, all that we love best,
Our hearts, our souls, are on those waves away,
  Those ravening wolves that know not ruth nor rest.

Think how they sport with those belovèd forms,
   And how the clarion-blowing wind unties
Above their heads the tresses of the storms!
   Perchance even now the child, the husband dies;

For we can never tell where they may be,
   Who, to make head against the tide and gale,
Between them and the starless soundless sea   .
   Have but one bit of plank with one poor sail.

Terrible fear! we seek the pebbly shore,
   Cry to the rising billows, " Bring them home."
Alas! what answer gives that troubled roar
   To the dark thought that haunts us as we roam?

Janet is sad: her husband is alone,
   Wrapp'd in the black shroud of this bitter night;
His children are so little, there is none
   To give him aid : " Were they but old they might."
Ah, mother, when they too are on the main,
How wilt thou weep, "Would they were young again."

She takes her lantern—'tis his hour at last;
   She will go forth and see if the day breaks,
And if his signal-fire be at the mast :
   Ah no, not yet! no breath of morning wakes;

No line of light o'er the dark water lies :
   It rains, it rains, how black is rain at morn!
The day comes trembling, and the young dawn cries,
   Cries like a baby fearing to be born.

Sudden her human eyes that peer and watch
   Through the deep shade a mouldering dwelling find :
No light within—the thin door shakes—the thatch
   O'er the green walls is twisted of the wind,

Yellow and dirty as a swollen rill.
  " Ah me !" she saith, " here doth that widow dwell ;
Few days ago my goodman left her ill,
  I will go in and see if all be well."

She strikes the door, she listens ; none replies,
  And Janet shudders. " Husbandless, alone,
And with two children, they have scant supplies.
  Good neighbour !—she sleeps heavy as a stone."

She calls again, she knocks,—'tis silence still ;
  No sound, no answer. Suddenly the door,
As if the senseless creature felt some thrill
  Of pity, turn'd, and open lay before.

She enter'd, and her lantern lighted all
  The house, so still but for the rude wave's din.
Through the thin roof the plashing raindrops fall ;
  But something terrible is couch'd within.

Half-clothed, dark-featured, motionless lay she,
  The once strong mother, now devoid of life ;
Dishevell'd picture of dead misery,
  All that the poor leaves after his long strife.

The cold and livid arm, already stiff,
  Hung o'er the soak'd straw of her wretched bed ;
The mouth lay open horribly, as if
  The parting soul with a great cry had fled—

That cry of death which startles the dim ear
  Of vast eternity. And, all the while,
Two little children in one cradle near
  Slept face to face, on each sweet face a smile.

The dying mother o'er them as they lay
  Had cast her gown, and wrapp'd her mantle's fold;
Feeling chill death creep up, she will'd that they
  Should yet be warm while she was lying cold.

Rock'd by their own weight sweetly sleep the twain,
  With even breath, and foreheads calm and clear,—
So sound that the last trump might call in vain,
  For, being innocent, they have no fear.

Still howls the wind, and ever a drop slides
  Through the old rafters where the thatch is weak.
On the dead woman's face it falls, and glides,
  Like living tears, along her hollow cheek.

And the dull wave sounds ever like a bell:
  The dead lies still and listens to the strain;
For when the radiant spirit leaves its shell,
  The poor corpse seems to call it back again.

It seeks the soul thro' the air's dim expanse,
  And the pale lip saith to the sunken eye,
"Where is the beauty of thy kindling glance?"
  "And where thy balmy breath," it makes reply.

Alas! live, love, find primroses in Spring!
  Fate hath one end for festival and tear:
Bid your hearts vibrate, make your glasses ring;
  But as dark ocean drinks each streamlet clear,

So, for the kisses that delight the flesh,
  For mother's worship, and for children's bloom;
For song, for smile, for love so fair and fresh,
  For laugh, for dance, there is one goal—the tomb.

And why doth Janet pass so fast away?
　What hath she done within that house of dread?
What foldeth she beneath her mantle grey,
　And hurries home, and hides it in her bed,
With half averted face, and nervous tread?
　What hath she stolen from the awful dead?

The dawn was whitening over the sea's verge
　As she sat pensive, touching broken chords
Of half remorseful thoughts, while the hoarse surge
　Howl'd a sad concert to her broken words.

" Ah, my poor husband ! we had five before—
　Already so much care, so much to find,
For he must work for all.　I give him more.
　What was that noise, his step?　Ah no, the wind.

" That I should be afraid of him I love !
　I have done ill.　If he should beat me now,
I would not blame him.　Did not the door move?
　Not yet, poor man."　She sits with careful brow,
Wrapp'd in her inward grief, nor hears the roar
　Of winds and waves that dash against his prow,
Nor the black cormorant shrieking on the shore.

Sudden the door flies open wide, and lets
　Noisily in the dawn-light, scarcely clear;
And the good fisher, dragging his damp nets,
　Stands on the threshold with a joyous cheer.

"'Tis thou !" she cries, and, eager as a lover,
　Leaps up, and holds her husband to her breast;
Her greeting kisses all his vesture cover.
　"'Tis I, good wife;" and his broad face express'd

How gay his heart, that Janet's love made light.
  "What weather was it?" "Hard." "Your fishing?"
    "Bad.
"The sea was like a nest of thieves to-night;
  But I embrace thee, and my heart is glad.

"There was a devil in the wind that blew;
  I tore my net, caught nothing, broke my line;
And once I thought the bark was broken too.
  What did you all the night long, Janet mine?"

She, trembling in the darkness, answered, 'I?
  Oh, nought—I sew'd, I watch'd, I was afraid,
The waves were loud as thunders from the sky;
  But it is over." Shyly then she said—

"Our neighbour died last night, it must have been
  When you were gone. She left two little ones—
So small, so frail—William and Madeline.
  The one just lisps, the other scarcely runs."

The man looked grave, and in the corner cast
  His old fur bonnet, wet with rain and sea,
Mutter'd awhile, and scratch'd his head; at last,
  "We have five children—this makes seven," said he.

"Already in bad weather we must sleep
  Sometimes without our supper. Now—Ah well,
'Tis not my fault. These accidents are deep.
  It was the good God's will. I cannot tell.

"Why did He take the mother from those scraps
  No bigger than my fist? 'Tis hard to read:
A learnèd man might understand, perhaps.
  So little, they can neither work nor need.

"Go fetch them, wife ; they will be frighten'd sore
    If with the dead alone they waken thus.
That was the mother knocking at our door,
    And we must take the children home to us.

"Brother and sister shall they be to ours,
    And they will learn to climb my knee at even.
When He shall see these strangers in our bow'rs,
    More fish, more food will give the God of Heav'n.

"I will work harder, I will drink no wine.
    Go fetch them.   Wherefore dost thou tarry, dear ?
Not thus were wont to move those feet of thine."
    She drew the curtain, saying—"They are here."

THE PARRICIDE.

TRANSLATED FROM VICTOR HUGO.

NIGHT came.   The organ that had mourn'd the dead
Was silent in the sanctuary.   The priests,
Quitting the high cathedral, left the king
Dead in sepulchral peace.   Then he got up
And girded on his sword, and left the tomb
(For walls and doors to phantoms are as mist).
He pass'd across the sea, the sea that shows
The domes of Altona, and Elsinore,
And Aarhus, with their towers upon its face.
Night listen'd for the steps of the dark king,
But he walk'd silent, being himself a dream.
Straight to Mount Savo, gnaw'd by the tooth of time,
Canute went on, and his strange ancestor
Thus greeted : " Let me for a winding-sheet,
O Mountain Savo, whom the storm torments,
Cut me a morsel of thy cloak of snow."
Him Savo knowing dared not to refuse.
Whereupon Canute straightway took his sword,
His sword unbreakable, and from the mount—
The mount that shook before his warrior form
He cut some snow, and gat himself a shroud.

He said, " O mountain, death gives little light :
Where shall I go to look for God ?"　The mount
With its obstructed gorges, and its sides
Deform'd and black, hid in a flight of clouds,
Answer'd, " I know not, spectre ; I am here."
He left the icy mountain, and alone,
With his brow raised, and white snow winding-sheet,
Beyond the isles and the Norwegian sea
Pass'd into the grand silence of the night.
Behind him the dim world went slowly out.
He found himself a ghost, a soul, a king
Without a kingdom, naked, face to face　.
With an impalpable immensity.　　　　.
He pass'd on, saying, ' 'Tis the tomb ; beyond
Is God."　When he had made three steps, he call'd.
But night is silent as the sepulchre,
And nothing answer'd.　Under his white shroud
Went on Canute.　The whiteness of the sheet
Gave hope to the sepulchral journeyer,
And he went on—when, suddenly, he saw
Upon that strange white veil, like a black star,
A point that grew, grew slowly, and Canute
Felt with his spectral hand, and was aware
That a blood-drop had fallen on his shroud.
His haughty head, that fear had never bent,
He raised, and stared right forward at the night.
But he saw nothing ; space was black—no sound.
" Forward," said Canute, raising his proud head.
There fell a second stain beside the first,
Then it grew larger ; and the Cimbrian chief
Stared at the thick vague darkness, and saw nought.
Still, as a bloodhound follows on his track,
Sad he went on : there fell a third red stain
On the white winding-sheet.　He had never fled ;

Howbeit, Canute forward went no more,
But turn'd on that side where the sword-arm hangs.
A drop of blood, as if athwart a dream,
Fell on the shroud, and redden'd his right hand.
A second time he changed his course, and went
To the dim left—there fell a drop of blood.
Canute drew back, trembling to be alone,
And wish'd he had not left his burial couch.
But when a blood-drop fell again, he stopp'd,
Stoop'd his proud head and tried to make a prayer.
Then fell a drop, and the prayer died away
In savage terror.   Darkly he moved on,
A hideous spectre, hesitating, white ;
For ever as he went a drop of blood
Inexplicably from the darkness broke away
And stain'd that awful whiteness.   He beheld,
Shaking as doth a poplar in the wind,
Those stains grow darker and more numerous ;
Another, and another, and another,
They seem'd to light up that funereal gloom,
And, mingling in the folds of the white sheet,
Made it a cloud of blood.   He went, and went,
And still from that unfathomable vault
The red blood rain'd upon him drop by drop,
Always, for ever—without noise—as though
From the black feet of some night-gibbeted corpse.
Alas ! who wept those formidable tears ?
The Infinite.—Toward Heaven, of the good
Attainable, through the wild sea of night
That hath nor ebb nor flow, Canute went on,
And, ever walking, came to a closed door
That from beneath show'd a mysterious light ;
Then he look'd down upon his winding-sheet,
For that was the great place, the sacred place,

That was a portion of the light of God ;
And from behind that door hosannas rang.
The winding-sheet was red, and Canute stopp'd.
This is why Canute from the light of day
Draws ever back, and hath not dared appear
Before the Judge whose face is as the sun,—
This is why still remaineth the dark king
Out in the night, and, never having power
To bring his robe back to its first pure state,
But feeling at each step a blood-drop fall,
Wanders eternally 'neath the vast black heaven.

WILLIAM DERRY.
CECIL FRANCES ALEXANDER.

PSALM LXVIII.

I.

RISE up, Lord,
And let thine enemies be scattered,
And let them that hate Thee flee before Thee!
As the dispersion of smoke-drift,
Thou wilt disperse them abroad;
As the wax in its weakness melts off
From before the face of the fire;
So our foes—the unrighteous—shall perish
From before the Face of our God,
But the just shall exult and be glad.

II.

Chant ye to God!
Sing psalms of praise to His name!
The awful Rider extol ye,
Who rides on the raven-black clouds,
By His changeless immutable Name
Of JAH—and exult ye before Him.
—A father of orphans bereavèd;

A Judge that gives sentence of good
To the silent life of the widow,
Is God in His holy abode.
—God maketh the lonely ones
To sit in a home of their own ;
He bringeth the fetter'd ones forth,
To places happy and free :
Only the rebels must dwell
In a land blanched white by the sun.

III.

1.

God ! when Thou wentest forth before Thy people,
Proceeding on Thy stately march
Across the desert steppes,
Trembled the earth and quaked :
Yea—the heavens dropped before the Face of God,
—This Sinai's self before the Face of God,
The God of Israel.
The free aspersion of a rain of gifts
Priestlike Thou wavedst to and fro, O God !
Thy heritage, forlorn and sick at heart
Thou didst establish.   So in that lone land
The armies of Thy chosen dwelt long years.
Thou with Thy goodness for the needy ones
Didst so establish, God !

2.

Suddenly His signal gives the Lord.
Those who tell, in every coast,
Tidings of great joy, and high
Annunciation of good things

Multiply, a countless host
Of women, full of glorious boast ;
Kings of armies fly—they fly
  Like the birds with fluttered wings.
She who kept the house that day
For her lord, at war away,
Shares the spoils of victory.
—Ha ! ye warriors, once so bold,
Ye lie down by the cattle-fold ;
And ye see in your homes beside ye a sheen,
Like the wings of a dove in the sunshine glint,
That are covered o'er with a silver tint ;
Her feathers all lit with a manifold
Vibration and shooting of yellow gold,
That passes, the woof of the plumes between,
To a colour of strange and paling green.
—When, from many a field of war,
Kings the Almighty scatters far,
Through our dark estate of woe
—As o'er Salmon's forest line,
Night-black where the shadows are,
  Shows that silver gleam divine—
Comes a sudden intense glow,
Like the gleam of new-fallen snow.

3.

Mountain of God ! mountain of Bashan !
Mountain of summits ! mountain of Bashan !
Why watch ye, with a scowl upon your foreheads,
  Ye mountains, with your summits arching grand ?
Here the mountain which our God hath chosen,
  For a habitation in the land,
  Yea—to dwell there while the ages stand !

Chariots of our God are twice ten thousand,
  Thousands told again and yet again :
And the Lord's Great Presence is among them
  Here in Sion, as in Sinai then.
Thou hast gone up on high,
Thou hast captive led captivity,
  Thou hast received gifts for men ;
Yea—for rebels, who allegiance owed,
That the Lord God may have meet abode.

IV.

Bless'd be the Lord,
  Day after day !
Whoever loads us with sorrow,
  God is our Saviour for aye.
This God is to us the God
Of Salvation—and of Him the Lord
Out of death are manifold issues :
  Surely He will bruise
The very head of His foes,
  And the hairy scalp of such an one
As walketh on still in his sin.
Saith the Lord, " I will bring thee from Bashan ;
  I will bring thee again
  From the dark, voiceful, depths of the sea ;
  That thou thy footsteps mayst dash,
    Red-wetshod, in blood of the foe,
And the tongue of thy dogs in the same."

V.

They are seen—Thy goings, O God !—
Thy goings, my God and my King !
  In the place which is holy to Thee.

First, went the song-men in front,
Behind, those who strook the strings,
In the midst the choir of the maidens,
　Who skill the tabrets to beat.
In the full assemblies, O bless ye,
God the Lord, ye souls
That well forth in living waves,
From Israel's fountain-head !
Benjamin's tribe is there;
Small, but his chief at his head.
The princes of Judah are there,
With their goodly company;
The princes of Zebulun,
And the princes of Naphtali.

VI.

Thy God assureth thee strength,
　Strengthen, O God ! Thy decree,
The things Thou workest for us,
Because of Thy palace, which hangs
　Dominant over Jerusalem.
So shall kings bring presents to Thee !
Rebuke the thronging mass
　Of the men who hold the lance—
The swarming horde of the bisons,
The young steers among the herds
　That are nations of mighty men—
Till they move themselves restlessly forward,
　With tribute of silver bars.
He has scattered the hordes of nations
　Whose will is the onset of war.
—Nobles shall come out of Egypt,
　And Cush—his hands in haste
　　Shall yet be uplifted to God.

VII.

Sing ye to God,
  Earth's kingdoms !—sing psalms to the Lord !
    To Him who rides forth
On the heaven of heavens eterne.
    Behold ! He gives forth His voice,
    And that a voice of strength.
  Ascribe ye strength to God,
    His loftiness is over Israel ;
    His strength abides above,
Where the thin clouds fleck the sky.
    Terrible art Thou, O God !
From Thy sanctuaries—Israel's God !—
    Giving strength and strong defences
  To the nation.   Blessed be God !

PSALM XCIII.

1.

THE Lord is crowned !
With splendour robed around,
Robed with strength His Majesty is found.

2

So the world may rest—it will not move, I trow,
Stayed upon the Throne that rests in the eternal Now,—
From the ancient days, everlasting Thou !

3.

Lifted up the floods, O Lord ! in anger,
    Lifted up the floods the voice they have.
Yea, the floods will yet lift up a stranger,
    More unearthly music with their wave.
        Grand majestic voices of the manifold
            Waters ! tumbling breakers of the sea !
        Grander, more majestic, on those old
            Eternal heights, the Lord, than even ye.

4.

Thy laws are made steadfast for ever,
The beauty of Holiness sits on Thy shrine,
O Lord ! through the stretch of the days that are Thine.

*PSALM CIV.**

I.

BLESS the Lord, O my soul !
  O Lord, my God !
Very great hast Thou been.
  Splendour and majesty
Thou hast put on as a robe,
Thou hast arrayed Thee with light
  For Thy lucent vesture of wear,
Outspreading the heavens on heavens,
  As the tremulous veil of a curtain.†
—He who archeth and layeth the beams
  Of his lofty chamber of Presence
On the floor of the waters above.
  —Who setteth the clouds
Thick-encompassing, dense,
For the battle-car of His march.

---

* " This beautiful Psalm is at once felt to be a poetical imitation of
the first chapter of Genesis. But the writer does not propose to give a
bare recital of facts. He wishes to found upon them the praise of the
Creator. As Moses divides the work of God into *six days*, the poet
traces *six pictures.* The *first* corresponds to the First Day's work.
God made the Light. But the poet speaks, not of the physical creation
of the light, but of light considered as a symbol of the Divine Majesty."
(Reuss, *in loc.*)

† בְּרִיעָה—from a verb which signifies " to wave and flutter."

—Who walketh on wings of the wind,
Who maketh His angels
As swift as the sweep of the storm-winds,
As strong as the flame of the fire.

II.

Thou hast built up the marvellous building
Of earth on foundations that shall not
Be shaken for ever and aye :
Thou didst mantle it once with the deep,
Sheer up o'er the hills stood the waters,
—They recoil'd because Thou didst chide them.
From the crashing voice of Thy thunder
They trembled and hasted away ;
Ascended the mountains,
Descended the valleys,
To the place Thou hadst founded for them :
The line of their border Thou settest
Which their proud waves must never pass o'er :
Must never return in their anger,
To mantle the wide earth again.

III.

Thou sendest in freedom away
The bright springs into the river ;
In the glens, the mountains between,
They walk for ever and aye.
They give drink to each beast of the field ;
The wild asses quench the fierce fire
Of the thirst that is on them therein.
Beside them the fowl of the heaven
Abide ; and out from among

The Apriling green of the branches *
They give earth the gift of a voice.
From Thy lofty chamber of Presence
   Thou makest the mountain to drink.
By the fruitful issue that comes
   Of Thy works, the earth shall be filled.
He causeth the sprouting of grass,
   Green herb for the service of man,
    To bring forth bread from the earth,
And wine shall give gleams of its gladness
To man's heart, and brighten his face
   Beyond all the richness of oil,
And man's heart the bread will uphold.
   The happy trees of the Lord
Stand satisfied, even the cedars
Lebanonian, planted by Him;
There the chirping birds build their nests;
But the good and home-loving stork—
   Her house the cypresses are.
The mountains, earth's high ones, uplifted
   Are there for the wild goats to climb,
And the crags are a refuge for conies.†

IV.

He made the wan yellow moon
   To mark the vespers for aye

---

* עֲפִי, *leafage*, from a root עָפָה, to be luxuriantly covered with leaves and flowers. (Aram. עֲבָא, Arab. عڤ. Cf. *April.* See Fuerst, " Concord. Hebr.," p. 852.)

† " This delightful picture of nature, just twice the length of the previous strophe, is more deeply interesting, because it is almost *unique* in the Old Testament. Oriental poetry in general, and even classical poetry is not in the habit of drinking deeply from this inexhaustible source of beauty." (Reuss, *in loc.*)

Of the times as they come in their order ; *
And the bright sun, that knoweth so well
His unfailing succession of sunsets.
Thou settest the darkness.   Comes night,
  And in it will creep
All the teeming life of the thicket.
The young lions roar for their prey,
And seek for their food from their God.
Breaks forth at his bright birth the sun.
They gather and muster themselves,
  And in their lairs they crouch down.
Man goes forth to his work,
  To his service until the evening.

V.

How many Thy works—O Jehovah !
  In wisdom all of them made.
The earth is full to the utmost
Of an ample possession of Thine :
And yonder, the sea that is grand
And wide with its infinite spaces.
There are moving things without number,
  The little lives and the vast.
There the stately ships walk on,
And there the whale Thou hast fashioned
  To take his pastime therein.

VI.

Hush'd in expectance all these
Look forth and wait upon Thee,

* To a religious Hebrew it was rather the moon than the sun which
marked the seasons, as the calendar of the Church was regulated by it.

To give them their food in its season ;
And ever Thou givest it freely :
Thou openest Divinely Thy Hand—
They are satisfied fully with good !
But when Thou hidest Thy face,
They are troubled, and restlessly shudder.
Their spirits Thou gatherest in,
They breathe out the breath of their life,
And unto their dust will return.
—Thou wilt send forth
In solemn procession Thy Spirit,
And the work of creation will grow,
And Thou wilt make young and renew *
The sorrow-worn face of the earth.

VII.†

His glory shall be through the ages,
The Lord shall be glad in His works.
If He do but look on the earth,
It trembles exceedingly sore.
If He touch the mountains, they smoke.
I will sing to the Lord in my life.
I will lift up psalms to my God
While my soul can call itself *I.*‡
My thought shall be sweet in His sight.§

---

* Literally, of the abiding continuance, the immortality of species ;
spiritually, of the resurrection of dead souls, and of the great renovation
ever in progress.

† " As the author did not wish to stop with the idea of the Sabbath-
rest, the seventh strophe is consecrated to a poetic peroration. It is
linked to the last verse of the first chapter of Genesis, which says that
God saw that everything He had made was very good." (Reuss.)

‡ Ver. 33. Literally, *during me.*   § ἠδυνθείη αὐτῷ, LXX.

I will be glad in the Lord.
From this fair earth the sinner shall cease,
And yet in the space of the years *
The wicked shall not be there.
Bless the Lord, O my soul!
HALLELUJAH.†

* The Psalmist strains forward in spirit to the great regeneration, the new Heavens and *New Earth*, wherein dwelleth righteousness.— "Ita ut vel conversi ad Dominum non sint amplius peccatores, vel si converti noluerint, dejiciantur infra terram, et ultra non compareant." (Bellarm. in ver. 35.)

† No Hallelujahtic Psalm is ever attributed to David.

PRINTED BY WILLIAM CLOWES AND SONS, LIMITED, LONDON AND BECCLES.